The Man with the
Little Dog

GEORGES SIMENON

The Man with the Little Dog

Translated by
Jean Stewart

A Helen and Kurt Wolff Book
Harcourt Brace Jovanovich, Publishers
San Diego   New York   London

HBJ

Library of Congress Cataloging-in-Publication Data

Simenon, Georges, 1903–
    [Homme au petit chien. English]
    The man with the little dog/Georges Simenon; translated by Jean Stewart.
       p.   cm.
    Translation of: L'homme au petit chien.
    "A Helen and Kurt Wolff book."
    ISBN 0-15-156933-9
    I. Title.
PQ2637.I53H5913   1989
843'.912–dc19   88-21875

Designed by Kaelin Chappell

Printed in the United States of America

First United States edition

A B C D E

THE BLUE NOTEBOOK

Wednesday, November 13

WAS LAST SUNDAY'S INCIDENT as important as I am tempted to think? It is really an exaggeration to call it an incident. A chance encounter in the street. An unknown couple in the Parisian crowd. An exchange of glances.

And yet, for the last three days, my mood has changed, and decisions I had thought final no longer appear so. I am not being dramatic or sentimental about this. I am just a very ordinary man among the countless millions of others who are alive, who are being born or dying as I write these words, not to mention the hundreds of millions of beings more or less like me who have walked on the same earth, breathed the same air, known the same seasonal rhythm.

I would have written in any case, but before last Sunday I only planned a letter, a longish one perhaps, addressed to nobody, since I have nobody to send it to.

Yesterday, however, after closing the shop, I went to the stationery store across the street to buy a school notebook. They showed me blue ones and pink ones, green ones and yellow ones. I chose a blue one, probably because of a patch of clear sky that on Sunday, at about three in the afternoon, appeared above the Panthéon.

My letter would have had a very different tone from what I now propose to write. It's true that I cannot tell what tone I will adopt tomorrow or the following days, or in the weeks to come, for I foresee that it may take a long time and that I will allow myself some respite.

On Saturday I had made up my mind. I was calm and composed, and I watched the end coming with a kind of irony, such as my letter would have disclosed. I wondered how to begin.

"I, Félix Allard, forty-eight years of age, living at Number 3ᵉ Rue des Arquebusiers, Paris . . ."

Should I have added, as though making my will, "being of sound mind and body . . . "?

Of sound mind—I could vouch for that, although I don't know what goes on in other people's heads and therefore find it hard to decide what is normal and what isn't.

That was the tone I proposed to adopt. A light tone, with touches of sarcasm here and there, sarcasm directed against myself and nobody else.

Now that I am slowly blackening the first page of this notebook, I am as calm as usual, vaguely smiling, but I couldn't swear that I am not feeling faintly disturbed.

Because of the couple I met on Sunday? It may be.

The best thing to do is to give a brief account of that day. I woke up as usual at six o'clock, and it was still dark. As usual, as soon as I stretched my arm out toward the switch, Bib, lying at my feet on top of the covers, started creeping up alongside my body, wagging his scrap of a tail. When he reached my face, he gave two or three joyful yelps.

Then we had a little chat. . . . Of course Bib doesn't really talk, any more than other dogs do. I do the talking, and he answers in his own way. For instance, when he's had enough of my early-morning effusions, he tugs at the sheet to uncover me and then springs to the floor.

I slipped on my dressing gown, thrust my bare feet into my slippers, and went toward the door. All these movements, performed every day at the same time, mean nothing at all, I know, to most people. Yet they take on the gravity of a ritual for a man living alone with his dog, particularly if that man, after weighing the pros and cons and after mature consideration, has decided to give it all up.

In the course of my life, I have known other habits, other practices. I have been awakened in the morning by the smell of coffee and the sound of my mother's footsteps in the kitchen, later by an alarm clock, then by the movements and the animal warmth of a woman's body. A baby's whimperings have roused me from sleep, or the patter of a child's footsteps in the next room. Later on . . . If I begin like that, I will never end, and I might give a misleading impression of harboring regrets.

I have no regrets at all, about anything, I hasten to say. And no shame either, although I know this declaration would shock some people. It's true, for the time being. I don't try to foresee what I'll think tomorrow, even less to what conclusion I'll come, if I ever do. The conclusion, after all, is irremediably the same for all of us.

Bib ran in front of me down the old unpolished staircase of rough grayish wood. We had only two floors in the empty house to go down, one behind the other. The enamel plaque on the second floor belongs to a small firm that makes artificial flowers, which, on working days, employs about fifteen girls. On the ground floor is a wholesale store that handles raincoats and other waterproof items manufactured somewhere around Montluçon.

5

There is no concierge, and no other tenants. Bib and I are alone every evening from six o'clock on and all day Sunday.

I unhooked the chain, drew the bolt, and turned the big key, which never leaves its lock. Bib slipped through as soon as the opening was wide enough to allow him to pass, and rushed across to the corner of the building opposite, where he lifted his leg.

It had been raining. Not heavily; just enough to darken the sidewalks and bring a breath of dampness to this tail end of night. I stood in the doorway lighting a cigarette; I always carry cigarettes and matches in my dressing-gown pocket. I wasn't thinking of anything. I wasn't looking at anything in particular. Bib and I, the street lamp at the corner, the two other lamps along the street—all were part of the setting.

Rue des Arquebusiers is not like other streets. For one thing, it makes a right angle. Starting from Boulevard Beaumarchais, it stops suddenly after a hundred yards or so, just where I live, and then goes on in a different direction, toward Rue Saint-Claude, where it ends facing other buildings.

On Rue Saint-Claude there is a church, St. Denis of the Holy Sacrament, whose bells I can hear. Or, rather, I ought to be able to hear them, but I no longer notice them.

Bib ran back and forth from one sidewalk to another, sniffed at the trash cans and the tires of the parked trucks, while, leaving the door ajar, I went slowly back up to the apartment, where I opened the shutters before lighting the gas stove and putting water on to boil.

Things had happened like this for nearly eight years— the first two years without Bib—and I did that morning what I had done several thousand times. I went into the minute *cabinet de toilette*, which, like the rest of the apartment, had a sloping ceiling, and, looking into the mirror, which reflected the light bulb, I ran the comb through my hair.

It has grown thin and turned a color I cannot get used to. It is no longer fair, but neither is it that silvery, silky gray that you see on some men my age. Mine is the drab, dirty color of old sacks, and the white skin of my scalp shows through.

I wonder if other people, as they grow old, experience the same surprise when they look at themselves in the mirror each morning. I see myself looking so ugly that I sometimes make a face at myself. Even though I have never been handsome, yet for a good part of my life I've been able to meet my reflection without repugnance, if not with secret satisfaction. I was tall and muscular, broad like all the Allards.

Have I grown shorter? It looks like it. My big body has become flabby, my face is puffy and unhealthy-looking, and my eyes remind me of a cod's eyes in a fish store.

Don't misunderstand me. I am not complaining, I'm not lamenting my fate. And it would be quite wrong to think I have any regrets about the past.

I am simply clear-sighted, capable of looking at myself in the glass and saying out loud:

"You're ugly!"

And sometimes adding:

"You make me sick!"

Without bitterness, without nostalgia, and, above all, without resentment toward fate or toward man's lot, I accepted things a long time ago. The word *accepted* is not quite correct, since I couldn't have done anything

7

else. I don't care for *resigned myself*. Let's just say that I learned to put up with things.

I heard the water boiling in the kitchen and I poured it gradually into the filter of the coffeepot. I had no need to go as far as the window to know that Bib, after sniffing at everything there was to sniff at, would come solemnly back to the house and push open the door with his head. After which, according to a habit formed right at the beginning, he would close it in the same way before coming up the stairs.

Bib was wet and had his rainy-morning smell. He threw a glance at the old stove, in which, since it was a mild morning, I had not lit a fire.

In autumn and winter, I light one every Sunday, because we spend most of the day at home. During the week, I light it only when I get back from work, about half past six in the evening. Did Bib know that it was Sunday, and was he wondering why today was different from other Sundays?

In fact, both of us ought to have been living our last Sunday on earth. I had made up my mind to this several weeks ago. In the beginning, I had not fixed a date. I had merely said to myself, when I looked in the glass in the morning, particularly while I was shaving:

"When I've reached a certain point . . ."

In my mind, this meant two or three months' respite. I know the point beyond which I don't want to go, but it is difficult to determine it exactly. I ran the risk, by postponing it continually, of finding myself one day without strength or will power.

I really thought, that Sunday morning, that I had found out everything about myself.

"Today, Bib, old boy, we're going for a long walk . . ."

I like to pretend that he understands whatever I say and answers in his own way, with his tail or his ears or his eyes. The word *walk* is one that he knows well, and he displayed his joy by scampering around excitedly.

I laid the table. I still put on a tablecloth at mealtimes, wishing to keep up a certain decorum, or, rather, a minimum of self-respect.

The sky was already showing palely through the skylight. Almost all the buildings along the street are warehouses or workshops, and few people live in them. And all of these must have been sleeping late that morning. Even on Boulevard Beaumarchais there were not many cars, since it wasn't much of a day for going out to the country.

It was a typical early November Sunday; I would have said a typical All Saints' Day if All Saints' had not already passed. It reminded me of the cemetery at Puteaux and the smell of chrysanthemums, and of walks in the Bois de Boulogne, years later, with a child's hand in mine.

The paper wrapping crackled, and Bib waited for his cracker. The saccharine tablets made tiny bubbles in my coffee.

Everything was as mild and drab as the sky, and in thousands of kitchens people were eating breakfast, too, and wondering what to do with their Sunday.

I knew what I would do with mine. I had to begin with my routine, which meant doing the housework. Nobody else saw to that. I could have afforded a cleaning woman for an hour or two every morning. My budget could have stood it, particularly since chance has made me almost wealthy.

Is it my reluctance to see a stranger touch my belongings and intrude, however slightly, into my life with Bib that prevents me from getting one? I'm not sure. I must admit that I get a secret satisfaction from cleaning out my burrow, as I call it, keeping it neat and tidy, making my bed, sweeping up the dust, washing the red tiles in the kitchen and the toilet with soapy water, and, once a week, polishing the floor of my bedroom and my "study." Besides, the wax polish smells good.

Bib follows me with his eyes, moves when I reach the corner where he is sitting, and from time to time I speak to him, saying whatever comes into my head. Like so many other people, I have spent part of my life with a woman. There were empty hours in the evening and on Sunday mornings, particularly before the children were born, not unlike this one, and when I try to recall what we could have said to one another, I find nothing very different from my conversation with Bib.

After a certain time Bib, too, demands attention. My wife used to ask me suddenly, as if waking from a dream:

"What are you thinking about?"

I don't believe I ever once told her the truth. Not because I felt impelled to lie, or to hide anything whatsoever from her, but because my answer would have meant nothing. The most commonplace of thoughts are connected with others, with ancient or recent memories, with fleeting impressions, and I have never felt capable of defining my state of mind at a moment's notice.

I am no more capable of doing so today, when I try to reconstitute that Sunday, recent though it was. It is now Wednesday evening. I am at home, in that study whose floor I was polishing on Sunday morning when Bib decided it was time for a walk. I have been writing for a long time, under the lamp, which glows warm on my forehead, and the ashtray is full of cigarette butts, the air thick with drifting smoke. Bib, lying in my armchair, is pretending to sleep, peeping through half-closed eyes when he thinks I'm not watching him.

To be accurate, to be truthful, one would have to remember every minute and convey its color, its rhythm, its sounds and smells.

Day had dawned, soft and gray, as I had expected, rather the color of a tombstone—but without any macabre implications.

I remember seeing Bib go to his basket of toys and choose a red rubber ball, his favorite, pick it up daintily between his teeth, and deposit it at my feet.

"Let's play!"

We played for a quarter of an hour, while, along the sidewalks, people were hurrying to Mass.

I HAVE JUST PAUSED for another quarter of an hour, again on account of Bib. He is surprised at being left in my armchair for so long, and I wonder if he has ever seen me writing, because it's years since I wrote a letter to anyone. I feel he is watching me, trying to define what has changed in my attitude.

My study is a narrow room and has a sloping ceiling with a skylight in it. Some people might call it an attic. Wherever possible I had put up deal shelves and, little by little, filled them with books. A table serves as a desk, and, in addition to the old leather armchair I bought at a public auction, the only piece of furniture is a rush-bottomed chair.

A quarter of an hour ago, Bib jumped down to the floor with a hesitant air, then, after rubbing against my legs, lay down on his back and pretended to be dead. This is a favorite trick of his, which, like his other tricks, he already knew before we met. I taught him nothing, not even how to shut the ground-floor door. When he lies down like that, his whole body stiff, it means "You're forgetting me."

Or else, "I'm feeling lonely. Pay attention to me."

As soon as I got up, he went to get one of his balls—he prefers them to rubber bones—and put it in my hand. After this he went to a corner and stood facing the wall.

Then I had to go into the bedroom and look for some more or less unfamiliar place to hide the ball. There aren't so many of them, because he seems to know them all. That's why he would rather play this game outside, on the embankment or in a square like Place des Vosges, where there's always some small boy who volunteers to hide the object.

"Ready, Bib!"

I had not originally pictured living with a dog. I spent several months in my apartment without any company at all. One evening, I brought back a goldfish in a bowl, and for a number of weeks I enjoyed its silent presence. I would even speak to it, as to a human being.

When I found it dead, I bought another, then a third. I followed the salesman's directions scrupulously. Nonetheless, my goldfish always died after a few weeks. That was when the idea of buying a dog occurred to me.

I took an afternoon off from work and went to the home for strays at Gennevilliers. I had not decided what sort of dog I wanted, and I might just as easily have come back with a cat.

When I went in, some of the animals jumped excitedly in their cages. Others ignored me. Most of the dogs were fairly big, some of them huge; there was even a Great Dane which seemed to have a glass eye.

My glance fell on a kind of miniature poodle, not very purebred, with a gray coat speckled with brown and squat little legs. I saw him stretch out on his back, as he has just been doing, close his eyes, stiffen all his limbs, and lie there like a corpse.

"That's a trick," explained the keeper. "He's trying to attract your attention."

"Is he young?"

"I can't tell you his exact age, but, to judge by his teeth, he must be at least three, maybe four. I wouldn't be surprised if he'd been a circus dog."

He snapped his fingers.

"Somersault for the gentleman, Clebs!"

The animal hesitated, watched me for a moment, then made up its mind to perform a perilous backward leap.

"You call him Clebs?"

"I call them all that, since I don't know their names."

A few minutes later, the little stumpy-legged dog was running along behind me on the end of a string. When we tried to get on the bus, I was informed that animals are not allowed to travel on buses or on the Métro unless they are carried in a basket or bag.

In a hardware store, I found one of those carryalls of brown canvas, the kind soccer players use to carry their gear. Borrowing a pair of scissors, I made two holes in it. Later on, I covered these with coarse muslin.

I did not want to call him Clebs, like all the others. That evening, in my bedroom, where he had already sniffed every nook and cranny, I tried a number of names on him, watching his reactions. When I came to Bib, he seemed satisfied. Had it once been his name? Or did he just like the sound of it?

Next day, I took him along to the bookshop, and Madame Annelet, who still got around, with the aid of a cane, exclaimed:

"Whatever is that?"

"It's a dog. He's called Bib."

"Have you just picked him up on the street?"

"I went to choose him at the pound."

"Do you mean to keep him?"

"Yes."

"And to bring him here every day?"

"Certainly."

She dared not protest, because she couldn't do without me, but she was not fond of animals—that was obvious. She looked me up and down several times, as if to take my measure and compare my frame with that of the tiny creature.

"It's funny . . ." she sighed at last.

"What's funny?"

"That you should have chosen such a very small dog, an old lady's dog. A psychoanalyst would probably find it interesting."

She is an old woman herself, and I, in spite of appearances, am a man of forty-eight. No matter. They got used to one another. Bib soon understood that any familiarity would be unwelcome and that he must keep his distance. At Madame Annelet's, on Boulevard Beaumarchais, he never ventures onto an armchair, still less onto the bed where the old lady spends a good part of her days. Nor does he ever lick her hand, or bring her his ball to beg her to play with him.

On other Sundays, I take my time preparing my lunch,

and I eat it by the window before leaving to spend the afternoon outside. Bib noticed with surprise that I did not light the fire, that I shaved and dressed earlier than usual, and that, at eleven o'clock, I told him:

"Get your bag, Bib!"

He went to get the brown carryall from the bottom shelf of one of the bookcases while I put on my overcoat and got my hat.

If I mention chiefly factual details, it is because of a kind of reserve or, if you like, a loathing of sentimentality. Actually, this Sunday walk was going to be a last pilgrimage for me. Let's call it a farewell walk, and say no more about it.

I was not unhappy, or nostalgic. I saw things as they really are, as though through the indifferent eye of a camera, and I saw myself, too, without pity or indulgence.

I was living through my last Sunday, and that was all. My father, my mother, my grandfathers and grandmothers before them, had had their last Sunday, their last Monday, their last Tuesday, and so on. That didn't make them saints or martyrs or heroes. As for choosing one's date, there was nothing very original about that either.

If I had earlier decided to write a letter "to whom it may concern," it was by way of a gesture, a joke, as though to thumb my nose, and also in order to unburden myself of a few small things weighing on my mind.

Are they still weighing on my mind? I doubt it. That's all over. I'm a quiet, respectable person. For Madame Annelet, my employer, I am Félix, her assistant, on whom she can depend, a man whose past history she knows, though she cannot get used to considering him in the same way she does the rest of mankind.

For others, the local shop people and the proprietors of small restaurants where I sometimes treat myself to a meal, I am Monsieur Félix, who lives at Number 3ᵉ Rue des Arquebusiers.

And for those who see me go past at a regular time accompanied by Bib, I suppose I am "the man with the little dog."

For a certain woman, I am an estranged husband; for a certain boy and girl, I am a father they scarcely remember and about whom they're not supposed to talk.

And for three other people, a woman and two other children, I am not quite sure.

The plane trees on Boulevard Beaumarchais had lost half their leaves. There were still few cars around, and we walked, Bib and I, as far as Place de la République, where we waited for a bus. When one stopped, I merely had to open the bag, and Bib jumped into it, just as the conductor was about to tell me that dogs are not allowed. It amuses us to wait like this for the last moment, and there are nearly always some passengers who burst out laughing at the conductor's embarrassment.

My original idea, on the previous day, had been to devote this last walk to Puteaux, where I was born and where I lived until the age of thirty, on Rue Bourgeoise, near the church of Sainte-Clothilde, which is being pulled down. Would that be too much like a pilgrimage? I had been back to Puteaux several times. I had also been past the apartment I lived in later at Neuilly, on Boulevard Richard-Wallace, and had felt no emotion. Is it absurd or romantic to say that I was seeking myself there, in vain?

Although I am not really old, there have been several Félix Allards, who appear to me to be increasingly distinct from one another. Some of them I can no longer recognize or understand.

We got off the bus at Place Blanche, and I let Bib off the leash. Along Rue Lepic I wished it weren't Sunday, so I could enjoy once more the pushcarts lined up along the sidewalks and the smell of fruit and vegetables and of meat in the butchers' stalls, and all the bustle of the market. Almost alone, we walked toward Place du Tertre, pausing whenever I felt out of breath.

Why my final goal was Place du Tertre I am unable to explain. The place is not connected with any of my memories or any significant episode in my life.

In spite of the lateness of the season, there were tables set up outside, covered with checked cloths, and a brazier was lighted here and there. Many people were already eating, people from the provinces, for the most part, and foreigners, whom artists were inviting to have their portraits painted.

"Do you want lunch?" asked a sullen waiter.

"Yes."

"An apéritif?"

I said yes again, and ordered a Suze. For years, I have drunk neither wine nor hard liquor, on doctor's orders. Why have I kept this up lately, since I had already made my decision? Out of habit? As an indirect method of self-punishment? Punishment for what? This morning I put saccharine in my coffee, instead of sugar. And yet I have sugar at home, for Bib, who doesn't have to follow a diet.

The choice of a Suze was more unexpected. I uttered the name without thinking, although I had drunk it only once in my life, near a village whose name I don't remember, somewhere between Le Mans and Angers.

I was in the car with Anne-Marie, a convertible, the

first I had ever bought. I can't say whether or not Anne-Marie was already pregnant with Philippe. The inn, just outside the village, looked like a small farm, with a huge sow in a sty and an orchard full of white poultry.

It was very hot. The low, dark dining room looked out on both the road and the orchard, where I can clearly picture the beanpoles. The proprietress was a potbellied woman in black.

"Can we have lunch?"

"Why not?"

"What can you give us?"

"To begin, some pâté with radishes and cucumber. If you want, I can open a can of sardines. Then I can fry you a chicken."

"That'll be fine."

"What do you want to drink meantime?"

Throughout one's life, one speaks and listens to sentences like that, and a few of them remain, for no reason, imprinted in some corner of the brain.

On the buffet I could see bottles, most of which bore labels unfamiliar to me. Two men sat with their elbows propped on a table—a cattle dealer and a farmer, I guessed—in front of glasses filled with a strange-colored liquid.

"What are they drinking?"

"Suze."

"Give me a Suze, too. What about you, Anne-Marie?"

"I'll try it."

It suddenly seems very odd to me that I tutoyered her, that we slept in the same bed for years, that two children, who will soon be grown up, have in their veins my blood mingled with hers.

Things seem important at the time they happen; then

one fine day you realize they have left no trace. I cannot visualize her face or figure in that inn, which seemed dark in contrast with the sunlight that beat so fiercely on the countryside.

We must have talked. What did we say? All that comes back to my mind's eye is the proprietress in the courtyard, among her ruffled poultry, catching one and then another, finally choosing one that seemed ready for eating, and chopping off its head on a block of wood. That was the chicken we were to eat, and a girl about twelve began plucking it in the midday sunshine.

Why did I order a Suze at the café on Place du Tertre? I did not ask for chicken to follow, but calf's liver with fried potatoes, and I drank half a bottle of rosé. Bib, who had eaten before we left, got his share of meat even so, and, because people were watching him from neighboring tables, he could not resist showing off with a few dangerous somersaults.

I had known Place du Tertre and Sacré-Coeur twenty or thirty years ago. If I'm not mistaken, my parents brought me here with my sister to "see the panorama of Paris" while I was still in elementary school, that is, before I was eleven years old. I imagine there were fewer tables on the terraces, fewer painters with easels set up along the sidewalks. But I had not come in search of memories.

I had wanted to spend my last Sunday in a different way from other Sundays, and the idea suddenly occurred to me to look down on Paris from the heights once again. The open-air lunch had followed as a matter of course. That was all. Bib wondered why I didn't hide his ball, but I had no wish to make a public spectacle of myself.

"Off we go, Bib."

I stopped for a long time in front of Sacré-Coeur, amid the crowd of people going up and down the steps, the vendors of souvenirs and postcards, the nuns, priests, and curates in charge of groups of Sunday-school children.

I stared at the roofs, which, under the blank sky, showed every hue of gray and rose-red. I caught myself automatically picking out monuments, like a tourist, and I thought of all the generations that . . . No. That was morbid! It was better to look at people's faces, almost all of them devoid of expression. Men, women, children . . . scraps of remarks, almost always the same: "Pity there's no sun . . . We could have seen as far as . . ."

Bib was bewildered at being taken for a walk so different from our usual Sunday walks, with their long pauses on park benches and gravel walks on which to scratch. He could see nothing but moving legs, feet, and yet more feet, through which he had to thread his way carefully.

"This way, Bib."

He thought at one moment that I wanted to go down in the funicular, and immediately looked at his bag, ready to jump into it. I chose instead to go down the steps, which other people were slowly climbing, most of them pausing to catch their breath every few steps.

Then I saw them. Dozens of couples must have crossed my path, but none had caught my attention. These two were climbing up very slowly and, seen from above, seemed even more oddly shaped than they really were. The man's head struck me first, a monstrously huge head, a hydrocephalous head, such as one usually sees only in medical textbooks. The skin was as smooth and pink as a baby's, and there was not a single hair. The protruding eyes were lashless.

Below a fairly normal trunk could be seen two tiny legs, so flabby they seemed to be dangling, and he hobbled along with the aid of two canes, flinging one foot to the right and the other to the left as if each step he climbed was a great achievement. With every step, he bent his head, and raised it afterward to measure the distance he still had to cover, as though the white mass of Sacré-Coeur up there was the ultimate goal of his whole existence.

He may have been thirty, or forty, or more. He was something outside the world of normal men. It was no doubt a miracle that he was still alive.

As for his companion, a swarthy little woman with irregular features, she wore braces, one of which, with iron fittings, reached her knee.

She kept one hand on the man's arm, less to support him, clearly, than out of affection, and each time he got up another step, she smiled at him, to thank or congratulate him for his effort.

Our meeting was actually very brief, although I slowed my pace and stopped long enough to light a cigarette.

When I was within three or four yards of them, they paused for a moment, and the man with the monstrous head and flabby legs asked his companion, in an amazingly light and gentle voice:

"You're not too tired?"

He smiled at her, a smile I have never seen on any human face, a smile that reminded me of the ecstatic faces of certain Buddhas, and she exclaimed eagerly:

"Oh, no . . . I'm all right!"

They looked at one another as though to rejoice in each other's happiness, and then they looked up at Sacré-Coeur. Finally they turned around, hand in hand, to look at Paris, which lay stretched at their feet and, at that instant, belonged to them.

I went past them without making a sound, and when I turned to look back, a few steps lower down, they had resumed their slow, laborious upward climb, with the cripple's fingers still holding the arm of the man with the lashless eyes.

Friday, November 15

YESTERDAY I WROTE NOTHING, and this left me irritated and disappointed. I am under no obligation to write in this blue notebook every evening. I have not made a formal vow to do so. I thought myself free, released. Yet the fact remains that when you've done something once at a set time, it becomes a habit, almost a duty.

When I had finished washing my dishes and had adjusted the stove for the evening, Bib looked at me questioningly. As soon as I moved toward my study, he ran in there ahead of me and, without waiting for my permission, leaped into my armchair.

I had indeed intended to write. I sat down at my table, I pushed the lamp to the right distance and opened the notebook at the page where I had left off on Wednesday. Did I make a mistake to reread the closing paragraphs?

"You're not too tired?"

"Oh, no, I'm all right!"

I sat there motionless, brooding over these two remarks. I won't go so far as to visualize those faces, those eyes. It was the worse handicapped of the two, an almost monstrous creature, who could only by a miracle have got beyond the stage of childhood, who was worrying about his companion.

What disturbed me and fostered my bad humor was the feeling of having been taken in. True, they had spoken these two sentences. They had stared up at the white shape of Sacré-Coeur as if they had been waiting for this moment all their lives. Then, hand in hand, they had turned around to look at the panorama of Paris.

But what happened after that? What had happened before? What happened every day and at every other hour? They had not taken the funicular, on purpose, perhaps, for self-mortification, or because of a vow, or simply to test their strength. Right up to the moment I lost sight of them, they had won.

A few minutes, a few hours of exaltation. Each of them, surely, transferred his personal joy to the other; each of them felt the need of a witness.

Pen in hand, I pondered sullenly, but found nothing to write. I would not, I could not accept the existence of such communion. At all costs, I wanted to reduce it to a commonplace phenomenon, and I searched my memory for moments of the same quality.

What will have become of the man with the baby's skin by the time he is forty-eight, my age? He'll probably be dead. But where? And how? With what thoughts in that huge head, what expression in those lashless eyes?

Will the woman with the braces be there still, holding his hand? And what will be her fate eventually? A little lame old woman in an attic like mine, only poorer, with a geranium in a window box for company instead of a dog, which she couldn't afford to feed?

The answer was vital to me, so much so that I regretted having gone to Place du Tertre for my lunch on Sunday. This letter would have been so much easier to write! I would have left without regrets, I swear. And, even more, without remorse. I felt sure of myself, and at peace. I know what I'm talking about, because I have had more time than most people to think about it, to put my thoughts in order.

As it happens, I have always mistrusted the "moment," striving as far as possible to imagine "what comes after." Isn't that what matters? Since Sunday I have been less sure of it. I have been wondering. Bib is not alone in staring at me with surprise, almost with disapproval.

Yesterday, Thursday, Madame Annelet called me up to the mezzanine several times, as she often does. As soon as I have served a customer and she hears the click of the cash register, she rings for me. From the floor above, she hears everything. A spiral iron staircase connects the shop with her room, where she spends more and more of her time in bed.

"What was that, Félix?"

"A woman bought a secondhand book."

We don't sell many new books. We would never have room to keep all the latest publications. The shop sign reads:

C. ANNELET
NEW AND SECONDHAND BOOKS
LIBRARIES BOUGHT

The C stands for Clarisse, but she dislikes the name as much as I dislike my own, Félix. My grandfather, after all, was named Désiré, and my grandmother Joséphine.

One morning, eight years ago, when I had been back in Paris and on my own for four or five weeks, searching for a way to make a living, I passed the narrow window of the bookshop. On the sidewalk, in a tray like those on the quays, lay piles of old books. A card had been stuck on the windowpane with tape:

It was the height of summer, and the sun cast the shadows of the plane trees over the buildings. A girl went past in a light dress, and I looked after her, wondering at the self-confidence with which she walked. A lock of hair curling by her cheek, her handbag clasped against her breast, patches of sweat under her armpits, she walked toward Place de la Bastille, and the world was hers to command.

I don't know where she was going, or what became of her. I pushed open the door, setting a bell to jangling, and stood for a longish time in semidarkness in front of the counter. Finally I gave a gentle cough, and then, at the back of the shop, a flower-patterned curtain was pushed aside, and a woman emerged from an inner room. She was elderly and had listless movements and a hypnotic intensity in her gaze.

The smallest details are still vivid in my memory. To begin with, that curtain, with its red flowers and green leaves on a yellow ground—hardly the sort of thing you'd expect to find in a bookshop. Through the opening I could make out a narrow room, with a window overlooking the courtyard, where a carpenter was busy, in front of his workshop, mending the legs of a chair. He is still mending them.

Then there were the shelves full of books, and more books piled up on the floor. What struck me particularly was the chaise-longue, upholstered in an aggressive purple, as unexpected as the flowers on the curtain.

As for the woman who stood there staring at me with

her black eyes, she reminded me of a fortuneteller, rather than of a bookseller.

I could not imagine her among other people in the street, although at that period she still walked without too much difficulty. Now, eight years later, I still don't know her age. She might be a woman of sixty, prematurely aged, or, more likely, a woman of seventy-five or eighty who has decided to keep on living and finds the energy to do so.

"I've just read your sign about the job."

She looked me over from head to foot, and did not seem to find it odd that a mature man should apply for a young assistant's job. She seldom seems surprised at anything. She watches, she tries to understand. And I realized at once that she must have experienced a great deal, known many men in every sort of situation, and that, without leaving her stuffy back room, she has never lost contact with life.

"The young assistant, eh?"

"I am only forty years old."

"Some of those years must have seemed like two."

I must have turned pale. I was sure she had guessed, and, resolved not to tell her any secrets, I prepared to go back to the boulevard.

With the indifference of a clairvoyant, she went on:

"Your affairs are no concern of mine. What I need to know is whether you know anything about books."

She had not said "about literature," but "about books," and this detail struck me.

"I studied literature for three years at the Sorbonne."

It was her turn to be somewhat taken aback.

"Have you been a teacher?"

27

"No. I gave up my studies when my father died, to carry on his business."

Most people glance at you surreptitiously or, if they look you in the face, try to assume a neutral or smiling expression. This woman, on the contrary, was scrutinizing me quite shamelessly, and I quickly guessed that she was trying to remember something.

"Have you put on a lot of weight lately?"

It was true, and I nodded.

"You used to live in Neuilly, and your name is . . ."

"Félix Allard."

There was a pause, and her lips twitched in a faint smile.

"Life's a funny business! Come this way."

She drew the curtain back a little farther, to let me through to the untidy room behind the shop. On a small table were tea things and some half-eaten toast, and also a pile of magazines.

"Clear the chair. Put the books on the floor, anywhere. I can't stand up for long at a time. That's why I put the notice in the window."

She was wearing a dark dress, much too wide for her thin shoulders. Her chest and arms were painfully thin, too. By contrast, her body from the hips down had thickened, and, when she lay stretched out on the chaise-longue, my glance fell involuntarily on her swollen legs, which she hurriedly covered with a red plaid lap robe.

"Have you gone back to your family?"

"No."

"In that case, I suppose you're by yourself? Have you found anywhere to live?"

"Right around the corner, on Rue des Arquebusiers. Above the raincoat shop."

"How do you feel about things?"

"I feel nothing at all."

"You haven't seen any of them again?"

"I haven't tried to see anyone at all."

This was only partly true. It depends on what is meant by seeing again. She lit a cigarette.

"Do you smoke?"

And, pushing the pack of Gitanes toward me:

"You're sure nobody sent you here?"

"I told you, I saw your sign as I went past."

"Are you going to try to make a fresh start?"

"It depends on what you mean by that."

"A job . . . friends . . . Perhaps a woman?"

"If the last, I would not be here."

It's hard to explain. We were exchanging commonplace and superficial remarks, but we had nonetheless made contact at a deeper level. It was not what we said that mattered, and if she was curious about me, I was equally so about her. The difference was that I was applying for a job that she could offer or refuse me, and that I had no right to ask any questions.

At that point, particularly because I had been admitted into that dubious back room, I felt an almost passionate desire to be accepted.

"If I understand correctly, you've grown used to living alone, and you can put up with it?"

"That's about it."

"It's the same with me."

She told me no more about herself that first day.

"I suppose I needn't be afraid of your pinching money out of the till?"

I merely smiled. Words were becoming increasingly pregnant with meaning.

"I suppose, moreover, that you haven't any great expenses. If I'm asking for a young assistant, it's because I can't offer much salary."

She was miserly—as I immediately guessed—not from love of money, but miserly as people are who have been short of money, who know what it means to have empty pockets and nothing to eat, who have experienced real poverty and are permanently haunted by the fear of relapsing into it again.

"You realize that most employers would ask for references?"

"It's usual."

"And that, on learning of your past, they'd be reluctant to hire you?"

"I've discovered that by experience."

"You seem to be a calm sort of person. I hate noise, and sudden fits of high spirits or bad temper. I don't expect to be loved, and I don't care whether you like me or not. People don't interest me. My ideal would be to live in an aquarium."

About everything she said, as about the expression in her eyes, there was something simple, frank, and yet aggressive. Actually, I now wonder whether it was not her use of the word *aquarium* that morning that made me buy my first goldfish.

"One more question. How do you manage about women?"

And, when I could not find an answer right away:

"I've got a maid, about twenty, a plump, saucy little piece, who can't see a man, even a man like you, without flirting with him. What happens at night in her room on the seventh floor doesn't concern me. One of these days she'll get herself pregnant, like the rest of them, or else she'll leave me to try her luck on Boulevard Sébastopol. What I won't stand for is cuddling and whispering behind doors. Have you got a mistress?"

"No."

"Do you pick up girls in the street?"

I merely shrugged vaguely, embarrassed by the way she was playing father confessor.

"I think we'll be able to get along together. There's no harm in trying—let's say, for two weeks. When would you like to start?"

"Whenever you like."

"Right away, then."

This was eight years ago. As she had foreseen, we got quite used to one another. I'd take an oath that, lying on her chaise-longue or in her bed, she can guess what I'm doing, and even what I'm thinking.

I sometimes secretly call her "the witch." For the last few months, she has seldom left her room. Her legs and feet have swollen even more. She can no longer wear shoes, or even slippers, and she almost has to be carried from one place to another.

As I have mentioned, her bedroom is immediately over the bookshop; it is just as untidy as the room at the back of the shop. The whole apartment is low-ceilinged, squeezed in between the ground floor and the second floor. It includes a bathroom no bigger than my own, a kitchen, a dining room and another room, used as a storeroom.

She has had five or six maids in succession, mainly Breton girls, like the present one, Renée, who is only seventeen. On the grounds that Renée has not got enough to do, Madame Annelet lends her, or, actually, hires her out, for a couple of hours each afternoon, to the third-

31

floor tenants, a young couple; the husband works for the Ministry of Justice, and the wife is a secretary to a lawyer.

Even in her bed, with an old bed jacket over her bony shoulders, Madame Annelet exudes astonishing energy. It is five years since she drove away her last doctor in a rage, shouting after him the filthiest words I have ever heard uttered by a woman.

Since then, she has followed no regimen, refused all medicine; she eats with a greedy, almost voracious appetite, and always keeps food within reach—toast, cake, candy, preserved fruit, anything that's edible.

She must have books, too, and she buries herself in them eagerly as soon as she has finished the weekly magazines, which she reads from cover to cover.

"Isn't there anything else down there about Marie Antoinette?"

She knows all the queens of old, particularly their love stories, and it's getting quite hard to find books to satisfy her.

"I don't care at all about war and politics, Félix. What I want . . ."

I know what she wants. I search the shelves. I come back with a pile of musty-smelling old books.

The outside of the shop is painted blue, like this notebook. I have a key to it.

It is my job, at eight o'clock every morning, to get the crank from under the counter and go out again to raise the shutter. Renée then helps me take out the second-hand tray and stand it up on the sidewalk, steadying it with a couple of wedges.

Bib has his place under the counter, close to the crank, and he has learned not to stir when a customer comes in with a dog. He merely sniffs the other animal's tracks when it has gone.

A bell has been fixed up to summon me to the mezzanine. Madame Annelet sees me emerge through the floor, head and shoulders and trunk, and sometimes I don't need to go farther than that. I tell her:

"A young man wanted a paperback edition of Montaigne."

She listens, not always bothering to look at me, and goes on reading and nibbling.

AS I EXPECTED, Bib has just interrupted me. He wants to play. He has got into the habit of interrupting my writing sessions. The first time, I showed my irritation, as I used to in the old days with my children when they demanded the same story every evening. Now, I have plenty of time, because my system requires less and less sleep.

I believe I wrote that, whereas Madame Annelet knows almost everything about me, I know very little about her. Once, however, a few months after I first entered the bookshop on Boulevard Beaumarchais, she told me something about her life.

"I've been married, too, Félix."

Her voice was hard, her eyes devoid of feeling.

"At thirty-five—just imagine—I took it into my head to marry a man named Emile Doyen, who was forty, about your age, and looked as quiet as you. His job was a quiet one, too: proofreader at Crescent Press, where he spent days or nights in a glass cage bent over proofs."

"Did you already have the bookshop?"

"Not yet. I was thinking, though, about starting a little business again."

No reference to what she had done before that. A blank of at least thirty-five years, which she never made any attempt to fill in for my benefit.

"I established it under my maiden name, since I'm a careful person, and I bought the stock with my own savings. One week, my husband would go off in the morning and come back at night; next week, he'd be on the night shift and leave me after supper, then wake me up at dawn."

Her monotonous delivery, her expressionless face, seemed deliberately to emphasize the uneventfulness of her married life. She never mentioned the words *love* or *affection*. There was not one picture of a man in the place; nor any picture of her or any of her relations, no snapshot taken with friends on a seaside or mountain holiday.

"It lasted ten years."

"What happened?" I asked politely.

"One morning, he sent a boy to collect his belongings, informing me by letter that he'd decided to ask for a divorce, that he took all the blame and would pay all the costs, and giving me the name and address of his lawyer."

I do not have Madame Annelet's insight, or, perhaps, her knowledge of life. I got the impression, however, that she had just revealed the crucial point, and I started from this to reconstitute her story. Was it true? Was it false? After several cross-checkings, I'm inclined to think that, except for a few details, it was as close as possible to reality.

"Do you know who he left me for, at the age of fifty? For a kid of seventeen, who sold newspapers in the street

34

wearing a man's trousers and an old jacket of her father's. As soon as he legally could, he married her."

"What became of them?"

"I imagine they're still together. She may have given him children, I don't know and I don't care. And he's probably still proofreading; they're a long-lived bunch."

It was not so much her words, as her tone, that struck me. Beneath the muted, deliberately even voice could be heard sarcasm and repressed hostility, at the same time, paradoxical though this may seem, as a kind of indifference or detachment, painfully acquired because it was vitally necessary.

She had certainly lied to me in saying that she was thirty-five and Doyen forty when she married him. The contrary was more than likely. From certain clues I figured she was then forty-five.

She was born in Paris; she often told me so, and I believe it. But I also believe that it was almost in the gutter, and certain phrases she has let slip suggest that it was in the Saint-Martin neighborhood.

Had she frequented the unsavory hotels in that district, outside which prostitutes pace like sentries in high heels? Or Boulevard de Sébastopol, which she often mentioned when speaking of her maids?

"When I was in Nice . . ." or "That reminds me of Narbonne. . . ."

She knows almost all the towns in the Midi, and she refers to them in a special way. She surely never visited them as a tourist; she has no relatives there; she has not brought back a souvenir from any of them.

When she was twenty, thirty, forty years old, brothels were still flourishing, and there was no suggestion of closing them. That is where I picture her, most convincingly, as one of the girls at first, and then as the madam's second in command, while she was still personable and attractive.

She did not speak about women in the way other women do. She had a more intimate, more physical acquaintance with them. One could sense that she had seen them stark naked, under a harsh light, hurrying to the washroom while the clients pulled on their clothes again.

She took somewhat the same attitude toward her successive maids. One day, when she didn't know I was on the stairs, I overheard her tell a little brunette, who only stayed two months:

"You had a man last night. You still smell of it."

Each of us has his own hierarchy, the upward path that is available to him. She followed hers, by sheer will power, from Saint-Martin to the brothels of Nice, Béziers, and Avignon, until at last, in her mature years, dressed in silk and decked with costume jewelry, she presided over an establishment in the neighborhood of the Madeleine or on Rue de Richelieu.

The final stage must have been to settle down and run a regular business. She must have chosen, from among her clients or elsewhere, a quiet, decent man who would bring her the necessary respectability. I don't exclude the possibility that Emile Doyen may have been found through an advertisement.

She got married, and her name was deleted from the police list of public prostitutes. She now owned her own bookshop, and lived there, with her own maid.

She may well have been beautiful once, to judge by the contempt with which she refers to other women's figures. Nor is she less critical of the male anatomy. She has obviously seen naked bodies of every sort and age and in every position.

But then, in due course, her face became wrinkled and her breasts pendulous, and her legs began to swell.

I may be mistaken—it doesn't matter, since I'm not harming anyone, and she will certainly not read these words. A woman with this background must have fought fiercely against age, rejecting it to the end, as she still rejects illness.

. . . Until that letter came from Emile Doyen, quiet, insignificant Doyen, devoid of passion or ambition, whom she had expressly chosen and who was leaving her for a little newspaper seller picked up in that gutter from which she herself had originally sprung . . .

I think it was then that she shut her windows. Literally and figuratively. She has purposely set her bed in a position from which the comings and goings on the boulevard cannot be seen.

What goes on in the world outside has no interest for her; she rejects its sounds and its smells.

If she understood me on the very first day, I may perhaps have the same reasons for understanding her. She has shut herself in. She lives only her own private life, enriching it with stories of queens, royal favorites, and famous courtesans.

I have referred to small details on which I base my theory. In the first place, I found, behind the books on the highest shelf, erotic books, which are sold only "under the counter." During the first two years, sometimes a different sort of customer pushed open the glass door, middle-aged men, for the most part, of a different social class from our usual clientele.

They would show surprise on seeing me, hesitate, and

ask, with some embarrassment: "Has the business changed hands?"

Or else: "Isn't Madame Annelet here any longer?"

"Madame Annelet is away for the moment. I am her assistant."

Sometimes I would say she was not well or tired. I could guess that she was listening, overhead.

"Can I help you?"

"No, thanks, I'll come again."

Then I would hear the bell summoning me to the bedroom.

"What was he like?"

I would describe him, and was convinced she knew immediately of whom I was speaking. She never pressed me, nor did she attempt to give any explanation.

At first I thought that the curtain between the shop and the room at the back had been installed at the same time as the chaise-longue, when Madame Annelet began to find walking difficult. On examining the curtain rod and screws, I discovered that they had been there for years and that the wallpaper behind the chaise-longue was much brighter than the rest.

Not only were the erotic books for sale, but the connoisseur could study them at leisure in that back room disguised as a boudoir. In Madame Annelet's company, or in that of a younger saleswoman, or a well-trained maid?

I don't know, and it is none of my business. Her life and mine have nothing in common except, at one time, complete failure, and, in the long run, a search for solitude.

Actually, we are playing a curious game together, spying on one another, each trying to guess the other's thoughts, as happened at first between Bib and myself, and as still happens occasionally.

She has no dog, no cat, no goldfish, not even a red geranium on her window sill. Only a maid, who, in her eyes, is no different from the naked, nameless girls she used to drive into the brothel parlor.

Thursday is one of my busiest days, because of the boys and girls who, on their half-day of school, come in groups or singly. I know them almost all by sight and some of them by name. Some are the children of local wealthy bourgeois and have an account, opened by their parents, to whom I send a bill at the end of the month.

And there is someone else who sometimes goes past the window, and I have long expected to see him open the glass door, but he never does. He lives barely three hundred yards away. Is it because he is aware of my presence behind the counter that he buys his books elsewhere?

Ten times that afternoon, as usual, the bell on the door rang.

"What was that, Félix?"

"One Stendhal, Garnier edition."

She is used to keeping a close watch on everything. In the old days, she probably asked her girls, in the same way:

"What did he ask you to do?"

I closed the shop later than usual, at half past six, going outside with my crank to lower the metal shutter after the secondhand tray had been brought in, with Renée's help. Then I carried the day's receipts upstairs. A smell of cassoulet came from the kitchen. It was very hot in the bedroom, and Madame Annelet's thin chest was almost bare under her bed jacket. After counting the notes and replacing them in the envelope, she remarked, without looking at me, as if it was a matter of no consequence:

"You're thinking of leaving me, Félix?"

Only then did she lift her eyes to mine, and I thought I read real anxiety in them. Surprised by her question, I did not reply immediately, and she added, with the curt laugh that she uses only in self-mockery:

"You know I hate strange faces."

She jerked her head toward the kitchen, where the maid was moving around.

"I don't care as far as the girls are concerned. They're all alike, and if I kept them too long, they'd become unbearable."

That meant that in my case things were different.

"What makes you think I intend to leave?"

"I don't know. I've been aware of it for some time."

And suddenly, to my amazement:

"When did you see the doctor?"

"Last time? About six weeks ago."

"What did the idiot tell you?"

Too late to draw back. The unexpectedness of the question caught me off guard. I tried to remain evasive.

"Nothing new."

"Which means?"

I had my overcoat on, since I had meant to go up only for a second, so I must have looked ridiculous standing there, tall and limp, with my head almost touching the low ceiling, in front of that bedridden woman with the dyed hair.

"How long does he give you?"

"A couple of years. Possibly three," I mumbled apologetically.

"Including everything?" She knew I would understand these words. Not two years before becoming an invalid, confined to bed, or taken to a hospital. No! Two years for everything; two years to the end.

I nodded, and I saw her shudder, her whole body tense with indignation. Raising herself on one elbow, she almost screamed at me, in a voice that had regained its vulgarity:

"And you were fool enough to believe him! Admit it, eh?"

"He told me . . ."

"Men are all the same. You believed him, I know, I've been reading it in your face for days. He's put that idea into your head, and I can see it gaining hold of you. Don't you know, you idiot, that one doesn't die until one wants to?"

It was no longer to me that she was speaking, but to herself, and she was quivering from head to foot. The tension was hardly bearable.

"Do you hear what I'm telling you? It's a matter of will power. Take me, for instance. I don't want to die, and I know I won't die until I want to, although I take none of their filthy drugs and follow none of their diets. But you, a great strapping fellow, you turn white as a sheet because a charlatan with a diploma tells you you have only two years left! And he must have said it quite seriously, the bastard, with a face like an undertaker's.

"Don't you realize that it's sheer murder? Next gentleman, please! Put out your tongue. Let's feel your pulse. When I prod you here, does it hurt? I thought so. And here? Aha! And your bowels? Oho! I bet you're breathless when you run for a bus. Undress. You smoke, needless

41

to say. You eat all sorts of junk, bread and butter, and sweet things. Not surprising! Lie down. Like that, yes. Don't move. . . .

"Oh, Félix, when I think that you let yourself be taken in like all the rest! You broke into a sweat; you watched the eyes of the man who was stuffing his rubber-gloved finger up your backside. He didn't? That surprises me. Those fellows love sticking their fingers up holes. . . .

"Two years, possibly three, on condition you give up smoking and sex, and live on unsalted crackers and noodles, eh?

"Doctors can go to hell, as far as I'm concerned, and I'll live to bury the lot of them."

She relaxed as suddenly as she had grown tense. Now she stared up at the ceiling and remarked, in quite a different voice:

"Were you going to do it?"

I didn't ask her what. I said nothing. She added after a silence:

"When?"

"I don't know."

I was crestfallen; I felt like a small boy. Then, once more, she gave her brittle laugh.

"That's better. Well, Félix, when you decide to, be kind enough to give me a week's notice, so I can find a replacement for you. And this time, I promise you, I'll make sure he's not a sick man."

Was it because of this conversation that yesterday evening I was incapable of writing in this notebook? On Sunday, in Montmartre, two scraps of talk had disturbed me so much that the whole question had been reopened.

"You're not too tired?"

"Oh, no . . . I'm all right!"

42

And on Thursday, the witch, in a fit of rage, had flung at me:

"Don't you know, you idiot, that one doesn't die until one wants to?"

Come on, Bib! Time for bed. Tomorrow is another day.

Saturday, November 16

2:00 A.M.

I HAVE DECIDED TO GET UP. Since I went to bed about midnight, I've been lying awake, and even when I grew drowsy, I still remained conscious. Even when my thoughts took the shape of dreams, I could see myself lying there in bed, flabby and unhealthy, under the sloping ceiling, and I could feel Bib's weight against my left leg.

I often drift between sleep and wakefulness like that. Some nights I look at the clock five or six times and figure out how long it is until morning brings back my routine and I can go and open the front door downstairs for Bib to run into the street.

At one point after switching off the light, I did in fact think about my dog. I don't like calling him a dog. I've been living with him for five years. He was thought to be three or four when I brought him back from the pound. He must be about nine, now, more than halfway through a poodle's normal span.

In fact, we're the same age, he and I. His back is growing stiffer, his body thicker, but he still keeps on playing with his balls and doing his tricks—pretending to be dead and, more rarely, turning back somersaults.

For a moment, I thought I saw him, on my bed, grown as large and bulky as I have, with his big head close to my face, peering into it with morose curiosity.

This was not the only unpleasant picture that passed through my mind. I remembered Madame Annelet, too, in her bedroom, raging against death. Everything she said about it, all her furious defiance, sprang from fear. Panic seized her at the thought of suddenly becoming an inert, decaying thing that people would shove underground as fast as possible to get rid of it.

Does she sleep more peacefully than I, who am not afraid of dying? Does she wait impatiently for the first signs of daylight? On Thursday evening, I was crestfallen in her presence, not knowing what to say, as sometimes used to happen to me with my father. I could see him, though not exactly as he used to be. I recalled the courtyard of our house at Puteaux, where I spent so many hours reading in the sunshine, with my chair tipped backward and my feet on the whitewashed planks.

"You're going to break that chair, Félix!"

I tried to picture my mother.

Why? Why? Questions, more and more questions, which I thought I had answered once and for all. But just as many are still pressing.

I slipped out of bed. I did not need to turn on the light, for the moon is almost full, and it is light enough in the attic for me to make out Bib's recumbent form and his half-open eyes.

At first he thought I was going to the toilet. When he saw me move toward the window, he hesitated, as I used to hesitate with my parents. He was torn between a selfish desire to relapse into sleep and his duty—I suppose he considers it a duty—to follow me.

I was fond of my father and mother. I have been "fond" of a number of people. What does that mean, exactly?

Before sitting down at my table to write these lines, I

just spent a quarter of an hour standing looking at the street, the buildings, the shop signs, and the three lamps. The sky is clear and cloudless. All day it was a smooth pale blue, with a cold sun that hardly cast any shadows. Now it is silvery, with a huge moon over the rooftops, and everything is a vast empty stillness, bathed in a neutral light that reminds me of the light over a dentist's chair.

The difference between Madame Annelet and me . . . I resent the place she has taken in my thoughts; I resent, too, the fact that she thinks about me as much as she does. I resent the way she looks at me, as if she guessed everything, without deigning to ask me if she's right or not.

My mother was like that, and as thin and dark. My grandfather Désiré Allard, taller and broader than I am, never forgave my father for marrying a puny little woman who played the piano and the violin, and I am not sure that my father himself did not come to regret it in the end.

Madame Annelet fought hard to pull herself out of the crowd, to secure a small space where at last she had nobody to consider but herself. Is she aware that five million Parisians are breathing and eating and working all around her, so close that, in spite of her closed windows, she's obliged to breathe their breath?

Does she ever think that, just as she's falling asleep, whole populations are waking up on the other side of the globe, that trains and ships and airplanes, twenty-four hours out of the twenty-four, are making their way through the darkness or the dazzling daylight?

She lives truly alone. I don't. With my forehead pressed against the pane, just now, I was staring at the grayish walls in the moonlight, the closed shutters, the empty balconies, and thinking of the human beings inside their boxes.

I needed no effort to picture another building, on Place des Vosges, three windows on the third floor, not so tall as the second-floor windows. I have never been in that apartment. It must contain pieces of furniture bought by me, carpets chosen by me.

As far as I can judge from the outside, it is not large— two bedrooms probably, besides the living room, the kitchen, and the bathroom.

The children are too old now to share the same bedroom. Unless he sleeps on the living-room couch, which would surprise me, Philippe must have a room of his own, which implies that Anne-Marie and Nicole, who'll be fourteen this month, must sleep in the same room.

Do they sleep in the bed that was Anne-Marie's and mine? The thought leaves me quite unmoved. I can see them in the same cold light that shines over the rooftops of Paris tonight. Philippe and Nicole are my children. Like other fathers, I paced the corridors of the hospital while they were fighting their way into the world.

There's another apartment about which I think, nearer, on Boulevard Beaumarchais, not to the right of Rue des Arquebusiers, like the bookshop, but to the left, toward Place de la République.

They only settled there two years ago—Monique, who is three years older than Anne-Marie, that's to say forty-three, Daniel, who is seventeen, and his sister, Martine, fifteen.

They live on the fifth floor, and a balcony runs across the front of the building, divided by a spiked railing, since there are two apartments on each floor.

Three human groups, if you can call Bib and me a human group. I'm forgetting the shop on Boulevard Beaumarchais, where, willy-nilly, I form part of Madame Annelet's group.

But the connections among them? I can't find the right word. I almost said the vibrations. On Sunday afternoon you could feel the vibrations between the two cripples climbing the Saint-Pierre steps, like those sent out by chords played on a large organ.

There they are in their various pigeonholes, and Renée, Madame Annelet's maid, in hers on the seventh floor. Each of them is breathing and dreaming, like Bib, who has just been waving his paws and uttering little whimpers.

Things aren't happening as they should. I don't mean in life, but in this notebook, whose pages I go on blackening in a depressed and irritable mood. My idea, when I started it, was to make everything clear, not only to others, if they should happen to read it, but to myself. I was almost sure I could do it.

I merely had to state my case, sincerely, cruelly if need be, in order to get at the truth. Doesn't each one of us, at some point in his life, feel the need to put things in focus? Doesn't each of us feel different from the rest, and suffer from not being understood?

Take any woman, the most intelligent, stable, and virtuous in the accepted sense of the word. Look at her with a serious and anxious air. I have done so; all men have done so.

"I'm trying to understand you."

"To understand what?"

"You must know; I'm not the first to have told you. . . ."

Whoever you are, you'll find her listening to you.

"You're different from other people. . . . There's something in you . . ."

It's just the same with a man, whether he's a genius or a fool.

"I'm sure that if you were to write the story of your life . . ."

A tiny little planet floating in a space formed of nobody knows what, among millions of other little planets, warmer or colder than itself, a minute individual, who'll soon be nothing more than material to be got rid of with disgust, solemnly undertakes to write the story of his life.

Of what life? Of his own private life, of course! Of what goes on in what he's pleased to call his mind.

At school, I was always being told:

"Félix, you're wrong to think you're cleverer than the rest. Rules are made for everybody. . . ."

They taught him, too: "You must love your parents."

And respect them. And obey them. They aren't just a man and a woman sitting in front of you eating their soup; they are a father and a mother.

As for Grandfather, he is a sort of patriarch, or apostle, such as you see in stained-glass windows.

"Show me your marks. . . . You've dropped down another place. . . . You're only fifth."

Fifth out of what?

"What's happening? Why aren't you working as well this year? Don't forget that your whole future depends on . . ."

And it's true. You have to choose a career, find a niche somewhere or other, on one floor or another, at Puteaux and Neuilly, in a cell of Central Prison at Melun or rooms on Rue des Arquebusiers. Or else, like Madame Annelet, work your way up from the brothels of southern and

southeastern France to a smart Parisian establishment
and the bookshop on Boulevard Beaumarchais.

One fine day, or one fine evening, you happen to be
sitting on a café terrace, or on a bench, or taking a walk,
with somebody you did not know the day before.

"What are you thinking about?"

"About you . . . You're a strange person. . . ."

"Strange in what way?"

"Do you often go for a walk with a girl and not say a
word to her?"

"This is the first time."

"Why me?"

"I don't know. . . ."

Because she is different, of course. And then she tells
you about herself, and you lose no time in telling her
about yourself, too. You each enlarge on what makes you
different: different skin, different nose and eyes and ears,
above all a different mouth, and you can't wait to taste
the difference; then breasts, and sex, and sighs and moans
all have to be tried out, for they are different, too.

"I love you."

"I love you more."

"I wonder how it happened?"

"It had to happen."

The horrible icy moonlight is growing quite poetic.

"It's a miracle. What would have become of us if fate
hadn't brought us together?"

"My life wouldn't have been the same."

"Nor mine."

"It would have been empty, like most people's. So few
know what real love is."

"How dreadful for them."

"Luckily they don't realize it."

51

"Do you think so?"

"If they realized it, they'd shoot themselves."

"You're amazing."

"I love you!"

I can hardly imagine such a conversation taking place between my father and mother, since it is of them that I am thinking. Still less between my grandfather and my grandmother.

"When there'll be just the two of us together . . ."

To be two together in a home, or a room, or a hovel. To go on talking about oneself, each considering his own story the most important.

"If you should ever stop loving me . . ."

"Don't talk like that. It's impossible! . . . The thought of being alone again . . ."

That's the point! Not to be alone. To be a couple, so as not to be alone. Why not three, five, ten, a hundred?

"Someday, darling, we'll have a child. . . ."

"Oh, yes . . . a child of our own! Can you imagine it? . . . Yours and mine! . . . Just our own!"

"I love you!"

"Me too!"

The crowd is no longer a hostile swarm, a mass of individuals each bitterly defending his own position. The crowd is a witness: faces turning back to watch a couple in one another's arms.

"Did you see that big man with the gloomy expression? The way he stared at us!"

"He was envious. . . ."

An old woman, smiling tenderly; a small boy, sniggering.

"What shall we call it?"

"If it's a boy . . ."

"And if it's a girl?"

"I want it to be a boy, and to look like you. . . ."

There are three of you. There are four of you. It drives me wild. Do you understand? It drives me wild that things happen like that, and that I need to write it down. There is a woman with two children on Place des Vosges. There's another, also with two children, under a roof on Boulevard Beaumarchais, which I could see from here if this house were a little taller. And for all of these I am, in a way, responsible.

For the past eight years I have had no contact with them. It is unlikely that they know I am here. Anyway, they never think of me. I don't exist for them; why should they exist for me?

"Responsible," did I write? For whom, for what is one responsible? Each of us does what he can, I like the rest, just as my boss—since I now have a boss—did what she could.

"And my grandfather?" a child will ask someday, in a world I will never know.

And a Philippe of thirty or a Nicole who will be a young woman and resemble her mother will answer:

"We won't talk about your grandfather."

"Why? Was he bad?"

What can they say? What do they know? Perhaps they'll get out of it with:

"You see, he wasn't quite like other people. . . ."

Perhaps that is why I want to know, and why I want others to know. I'm doing this badly. I'll be awkward to the end of my days. Meanwhile, it's cold. I am not sleepy. I have no wish to go back to bed. I'll relight the fire, make myself a cup of coffee, sit down in front of this table again, and, probably, spend the rest of the night here.

I hate that moon hanging just over my head, directly above the skylight. I hope it will soon move away and that I won't see it any more.

No, Bib, it's not time to get up. Don't pay any attention to your master. Go to sleep. Good dog!

ONE MAY MORNING, about eleven o'clock, I came out of Central Prison with a suitcase in my hand, and found myself in the square in front of Melun's Notre-Dame, having for more than four years seen only its rooftops and towers. The air was fresh, the sun already warm, and the first person I encountered was an old man with a white mustache wearing a Panama hat.

I was neither bewildered nor excited. I mostly stared at the pavement, the sidewalks, the buildings, listened to the sound of footsteps. Then, crossing the square, I went into a clean little café at the corner of a narrow street. Behind the counter, the proprietor, in shirt sleeves and a blue apron, was arranging his bottles.

I could just as well have been in a bistro in Puteaux or the Latin Quarter. The smell, the color of the floor and the few tables, the notice about not being drunk and disorderly, stuck up on the wall between advertisements for apéritifs, all were the same.

"A glass of white wine."

"Dry?"

"Yes."

I had not come for the sake of the white wine. I had come to renew contact, and the proprietor realized this. Without having seen me cross the square, he knew where I had come from. He'd served others like me. I don't know how he recognized us—by our pallor, perhaps, or the look in our eyes.

"Well, it wasn't too bad, was it?"

I said no. It was true. Time had not seemed long for me, and I wonder, in retrospect, whether it did not seem shorter than at any other period of my life.

"From Paris?"

"Yes."

"Nobody to meet you?"

"No."

I thanked him, for nothing in particular, maybe for having spoken to me; then I paid for my drink and made my way toward the station, pausing a moment on the bridge to watch the waters of the Seine flow by.

I didn't have enough curiosity to turn back and look at my prison for a last time, or to try and pick out the roof of my section.

At the station I had a long wait for a train, and I took advantage of it to eat a ham sandwich and drink another glass of white wine.

It was then, I believe, that I understood that I no longer looked at things and people in the same way. I had foreseen this; now I was experiencing it. I saw men and women, faces and hands, carts, luggage, freight cars standing on the tracks, lilacs in bloom in a garden. I heard sounds and voices. I recognized the smell of sandwiches, of beer drawn from the barrel, of wine and alcohol. But I stayed detached. It was all something outside me and did not concern me.

True, there was nobody to meet me when I came out of prison. But were all those who had left before me so desperately anxious to find somebody waiting at the gate?

Possibly out of vanity, in some cases, just as certain people like to be seen off or met at the station.

Through the train window I saw familiar landscapes once again: a stretch of the Seine here and there, a lock with boats, a fisherman with his rod at the foot of an embankment, gravel quarries. It's the line to the Côte d'Azur; I had often traveled on the Blue Train, and on the return journey it was at Melun that the wagon-lits waiters used to wake us up with coffee.

It might be supposed that I was full of plans, that I'd had plenty of time to sketch out my future. The contrary is true. I was as blank as an empty page, indifferent to everything except ridiculous details, such as the newspaper my neighbor was reading, the conversation of two soldiers on leave, some market gardeners glimpsed for a moment in a huge plot irrigated by a score of sprinklers.

There are plenty of hotels around the Gare de Lyon, but I have always disliked the neighborhood of stations. You are not really inside the town, or else you are no longer in it, and yet you don't feel you are anywhere else.

I had no reason to choose one district rather than another. I know nobody at Puteaux now. Neuilly is nothing but a memory, and I sometimes wonder whether it was really I who lived there.

I walked straight ahead, as I would have done if I'd arrived at the Gare du Nord or the Gare Montparnasse. I found myself beside the river, and I walked along the Arsenal dock and finally reached the Bastille.

I began looking at the signs of the cheaper hotels, because my suitcase, which I kept shifting from one hand to the other, was beginning to feel heavy. Eventually, I went into the narrow white-painted entrance of a hotel on Rue Castex, close to Rue Saint-Antoine.

The landlady, wiping her pudgy hands, scanned me closely. I had not noticed before that human beings watch one another suspiciously before making contact. There is a pause, while furtive glances are exchanged.

"For one night?"

"I'd rather have a room by the week or the month, if it's not too expensive."

"Are you French?"

"Yes."

"You're alone?"

"Yes."

Something about me worried her, something she could not figure out, but she nonetheless showed me a room overlooking the courtyard. I went to get something to eat on Rue Saint-Antoine, and drank yet another glass of white wine. Then I lay down, fully dressed, and was surprised on waking to find that night had fallen.

I spent a whole week walking around, venturing a little farther each time—now taking the bus to Place de l'Opéra, another time to Châtelet, and so on. . . . It did not rain once all that week. In that fair weather, women wore light, bright-colored spring dresses. I had forgotten the special way women walk when they have just shed their winter clothes, as if they derived a kind of sexual excitement from this state of undress, which makes them unconsciously provocative.

On Monday or Tuesday, I finally found myself in the reception room of Maître Forniol, my lawyer, who lives in an imposing but comfortable building on Boulevard Haussmann. I recognized the secretary, whom he already had at the time of my trial. Have I changed so much that she failed to recognize me?

"Have you an appointment?"

"No."

She handed me a pad and pencil: name, purpose of visit, with dotted lines for the answers, just as in a government office. I merely signed my name.

"I think that will be enough," I said.

She read my name without surprise or curiosity, as if it suggested nothing to her.

"I'm afraid you may have to wait some time. Maître Forniol is in conference."

In the old days I, too, had always been in conference when certain people called.

"I'll wait."

I sat alone in the reception room, and stayed there doing nothing. That's something I have learned: how not to move, to remain perfectly blank. I heard the telephone ringing, the secretary's voice, and a man's voice, muffled, behind a baize door.

A law clerk came through, carrying files under his arm, a young man I did not know. He seemed surprised to find somebody there.

"Are you waiting for Maître Forniol?"

"Yes."

"Has his secretary seen you?"

"Yes."

What made him frown as he looked at me? I had no spots on my nose or smut on my face. I was respectably dressed, waiting motionless in my chair.

He went through the baize door, which, a little later somebody, whom I could not see from where I was, pushed open enough to glance at me. At last the secretary, Mademoiselle Emma, or Irma, I forget which, came to get me.

"Maître Forniol will see you now."

She took me into the office, which was empty, showed me to a chair, and disappeared. In the next room, the door of which was ajar, somebody was talking.

"Don't worry, my dear fellow . . . I'll ask for two weeks' adjournment, which will give us time to work on you know who. . . . Yes, yes, of course! . . . You can depend on it. . . . Our opponents can't attempt anything before . . ."

He was speaking into the telephone in exactly the same voice he had used to me four years earlier.

"No. Unfortunately, I have no free evening this week, but please give my wife's kind regards to yours. . . . Above all, don't do anything. Wait till you hear from me. . . . It'll be all right. . . ."

The same words, too, as near as made no difference. Now he was whispering to somebody, and a few minutes later he came in, quite unlike his voice, with the serious and preoccupied air of a man overburdened with responsibilities.

He has not changed at all. He is still younger and dapper. I stood up, because at Melun you acquire the habit of standing up as soon as the door opens.

He glanced at me, and could not restrain a look of surprise.

"So, I see you've got out . . ." he began.

He made a mental calculation as he sat down behind his desk.

"In fact, you've had your sentence remitted? If I'm not mistaken, you were to have been released in . . ."

"Six months."

He did not ask how I was; still less did he bother to simulate cordiality.

"My secretary will have told you that I'm . . ."

"Extremely busy. I won't waste your time."

My presence seemed to disturb or embarrass him. Yet at the assize court he had defended me with fervor, even with passion.

"What can I do for you?"

I wondered if he was going to pull out his wallet.

"Are the children still living with my wife?"

He became even more guarded, as though I really were becoming an adversary.

"Why do you ask that?"

"Does it surprise you?"

He took his time, fiddling with an ivory paper knife and looking at me with some annoyance.

"Look here, Allard . . . I needn't remind you of your position, and I suppose the papers were sent to you in due course. . . ."

I remained calm and expressionless. It was he who was put out. He began pulling at his ear lobe.

"Your wife has not asked for a divorce, as she could have, in order not to have a different name from her children. . . ."

"Even if we were divorced, I would have authorized her to keep mine."

He glanced at me severely, shocked at my daring to make such a remark. In his opinion, I ought not to be here; I should have had the decency to disappear and, above all, to keep quiet.

"The fact remains that she merely asked for a separation order. Subsequently, on the advice of one of my colleagues, she insured her peace of mind by requesting that you forfeit your paternal rights, by virtue of the law of July 24, 1889. . . ."

I did not bat an eyelid. Why should I, since I already

60

knew this? Forfeiture of paternal rights. Law of July 24, 1889, Article 2. Perhaps he was refreshing his memory when he was muttering in the next room a few minutes before.

He concluded, throwing up his hands:

"Under the circumstances . . ."

"Do you know where they live?"

He picked up the paper knife again.

"I can tell you that I know where Madame Allard and her children are living. I saw them less than two months ago, and they are quite well. Now, if you'll excuse me, I'm due in court."

"You refuse to give me their address?"

"Why do you want it? You have no legal or moral right to disturb their existence, and, for my part, I consider myself bound to . . ."

"I have nothing to say to Anne-Marie. I don't want to see her, or discuss anything at all with her. Nor do I intend to confront the children and announce to them: I'm your father. . . ."

I did not raise my voice. I was neither angry nor disheartened. Those words, too, have lost all meaning for me.

"But from time to time, with all possible prudence, I might want to see the children from a distance. Since, according to you, this can't be done, I'll make inquiries elsewhere. . . ."

I suppose it was my calmness, my absence of emotion that impressed him, added to the fact that he was in a hurry and was afraid I'd detain him by my insistence.

"Will you give me your word that this is really your intention and that you won't go any further?"

I rose from my chair.

"You don't need my word. You're forgetting about the forfeiture of paternal rights. . . ."

"If I reminded you of that . . ."

"You had every right to do so."

"Listen . . ."

He rose, too, and showed me to the door, muttering: "Forget about this visit. I haven't seen you. They live at 23 Place des Vosges."

"They don't need anything?"

"Nothing at all."

"Is she working?"

"You're asking too many questions, and I'm already ten minutes late. Excuse me. I've still got to make a telephone call."

He did not shake hands with me.

"Irma, be kind enough to show Monsieur . . . out."

Irma was her name, then. As for mine, he left it unmentioned, merely leaving a pause.

Ten days earlier, I had chosen a small hotel on Rue Castex, near the corner with Rue Saint-Antoine, and now I had discovered that Anne-Marie was living on Place des Vosges with the children. Four hundred yards away, five hundred maybe? It didn't matter.

Forniol need not worry. Philippe was eight years old then; Nicole, six. I saw them at a distance, being taken to school by a maid.

And I also saw Anne-Marie, who now owned a small green car and who, apart from having cut her hair, had scarcely changed. She was working at that time at a couturier's on Faubourg Saint-Honoré, and since then has opened her own boutique, near St. Philippe-du-Roule.

I never felt tempted to get closer to them, still less to make myself known. If I happen to speak of them now, as night is drawing to a close and the time has almost come to open the door for Bib, it is in order to return indirectly to the subject of myself.

I was not interested in eight-year-old Philippe, still less in his sister.

"They're your children. . . ."

They are Anne-Marie's, too. And there was a time, indeed, when we thought the world of them.

"He has your nose. . . ."

"Maybe my nose, but he has your expression. . . ."

Mine, yours—it always comes back to that. I once saw, in a documentary film, millions of spermatozoa struggling ferociously to be the first to pierce the ovum. One of them won; the others were wasted.

From that battle, a child was born. My children, then—since they are mine—go to school with other children who have their grandfather's or grandmother's nose or expression.

I turned my attention to finding somewhere to live, and I happened to discover this place, which is just right for me, in a district of warehouses and small workshops that reminds me of Puteaux.

To the left, on my street, are the Réunis warehouses, which own at least twenty trucks. Then there is a candlestick maker's. Opposite my place is a cheap restaurant, with a façade painted sky blue and its name: CHEZ ROSE.

One day I read the sign in the bookshop window, and little by little I organized my life. I had put on weight at Melun, which was nobody's fault, not even that of prison regulations. I continued putting on weight, and looking puffier and uglier, particularly in the morning, but I felt all right.

I had no desire for anything, not even for contact with

people. I had reached a state of serenity. Having asked myself questions, I had eventually answered them in a way that satisfied me. It was pointless to return to them.

This did not prevent me from going, now and then, to sit on a bench in Place des Vosges, from which I could occasionally catch sight of the children.

Winter came, and summer, longer days, shorter days, different fruit and vegetables on the barrows on Rue Saint-Antoine and the open-air market on Boulevard Richard-Lenoir, overcoats or jackets, Easter holidays, summer vacations, beginning of school. Suddenly we would be selling books about shooting or cooking game, or people would be ordering Christmas cards. And as the years went by, Madame Annelet spent less and less time up and about, and ate more and more.

I don't intend any irony. I went on preparing my morning coffee, feeding my goldfish, which was doomed to die nonetheless, and which would have been most surprised to learn that a dog would shortly take its place. And who's going to take *my* place, in *my* goldfish bowl?

Philippe started going to the Lycée Turgot, on Rue de Turbigo. His appearance changed, his way of walking, his expression. He grew taller and thinner, and had the prominent bones I had at his age.

This was the time when he must be growing aware of his own existence. At any rate, for me it was at his age that I first made the discovery.

In a very short time, during which I had chosen a dog at Gennevilliers, sold books, raised the shutter in the morning, got used to new maids, and carried the day's receipts up to Madame Annelet, Philippe had turned sixteen. He is now preparing for his baccalaureate, his secondary-school certificate. For his last birthday his mother bought him a motorbike. The first few days, he never got tired of buzzing like a big fly around the railings of Place des Vosges.

He has bought himself a leather jacket. On Thursdays, he joins a group of boys and girls at a café near Place de la République, where there are only young people, drinking fruit juice and listening to the jukebox.

I used to have a bicycle to get to the Lycée Pasteur, in Neuilly, since there was no such school in Puteaux.

I . . . I . . .

I watch Philippe, and I also watch Daniel, who entered the same school as Philippe when, with his mother and sister, he came to live on Boulevard Beaumarchais.

Daniel, who is a year older, is in a different class. He belongs to a different group. I don't know whether they know each other. I compare; I observe; I keep hidden; I wonder. . . .

Six o'clock. Bib has sensed this and jumped off the bed. The fire has gone out again. After I've been down to open the door, I'll heat some water for coffee. . . .

Sunday, November 17

11:00 A.M.

THE RAIN HAS BEEN FALLING hard since midday yesterday, in great cold drops, blackening the building fronts, pouring down the windowpanes, choking the drainpipes. Wherever you look, the sky is thick, and it's so dark that this morning lights are on everywhere.

I'm quite happy when it rains on Sunday. Not because I envy the people who, at the first gleam of sun, rush off into the country. I used to have a car—even several, at one time. I know the roads to Deauville and Le Touquet, the roads to the South, and the best places to eat on the way. I envy nobody.

If I don't dislike seeing it rain when people have the day off, it is because then I can feel that all pigeonholes are full, the houses brimming over with human life.

Yesterday evening, Bib and I had been almost alone as we walked along the sidewalks, except for an occasional figure darting from the door of a building to a waiting car, which promptly drove off.

The movie theaters must have been crowded, and the restaurants and dance halls, and no doubt resigned processions under umbrellas were pacing up and down in front of the brightly lit entrances on the Champs-Elysées and the Grands Boulevards.

There were some blank spaces on the apartment-house

façades, some darkened windows, some empty homes. Daniel, hugging the walls, had made his way to the Métro. I suppose he was going to the movies. His mother and sister stayed in their apartment, where, at eleven o'clock, the lights were still on. I don't know what they were doing.

On Place des Vosges, nobody else went out. Several cars were parked along the curbs, and I saw one draw up and a young couple get out. Was there a party on the third floor? It's quite likely, because the shadows passing to and fro behind the curtains seemed to be those of people dancing.

I went back to Boulevard Beaumarchais and stood for a while, sheltering in a doorway, in the hope of seeing Daniel come home. Bib, who was soaked, eventually put on such a miserable expression that I abandoned my post.

This morning, we went out again, without hurrying, walking at a steady pace along empty streets. Sometimes I caught a glimpse of a face behind net curtains; somebody was watching us and wondering what we were doing in the rain.

I suppose many people have taken advantage of the rain to sleep, those who have no children to wake them at the crack of dawn. Others listen half-heartedly to the radio, which is indistinguishable from that in the apartment next door or that on the floor above. One thing I'm certain of: Philippe is not reading a book.

I was thinking about him as I sat on a wet bench far enough from his window for his mother not to recognize me if she should happen to look out. I have never seen Philippe with a book other than his schoolbooks. Daniel is different, and I'd bet that last night he didn't go to a local movie house, or to one of the big ones that show the latest pictures, but to some film society or avant-garde theater.

The drops of rain hit the sidewalk so violently that they bounce back, and water gets into one's shoes, soaking socks and trouser cuffs. I have put my overcoat to dry by the fire, where Bib is drying himself, too. He is feeling cross. I am not; but neither am I cheerful. I don't feel like singing. Have I ever felt like singing? My mood is one of quiet contentment, as with certain forms of physical pain that one eventually comes to enjoy.

It often rained when I was a child. . . . That's an idiotic remark. I mean that when I cast my mind back I remember a lot of rain, days like today, when the whole family stayed home, particularly when I was very young, when we had not yet aquired our van or central heating, and the cold obliged us all to take refuge in the only warm room.

Will Philippe and Daniel and the two girls retain as few memories of their early childhood as I have? And yet I have been told I was a lively, quick child, given to asking awkward questions.

I was born in January 1915, at the at the height of the First World War. My father, then thirty, was a building contractor and was called up to help construct the defenses of Paris. Louise, my sister, was born two years later, while the war was still on.

We were living in the same old house, with my grandfather, my grandmother, and one of my aunts, Léonore, who was not married.

I gather that my grandmother was a handsome woman, buxom, in the taste of the time. She was the daughter of an inkeeper at Chatou, where my grandfather, who was then a foreman, used to go boating on Sundays.

There is a family album with brass corners containing their portraits, along with those of uncles, aunts, and cousins I do not know. At Chatou, my grandmother was know as "la belle Joséphine."

Hers must have been the first death in the family in my lifetime. I was about four. I remember only the ringing of the altar boy's bell when, at nightfall, the priest came to administer extreme unction.

I know nothing about the funeral, but I watched the undertakers' men removing the black, silver-trimmed hangings. I can also remember seeing, that afternoon, men in their Sunday best in the seldom-opened parlor. They were drinking brandy out of tiny glasses—I can still smell it—and smoking cigars, and they soon sent me out of the room.

My grandfather was among them. Somebody said:

"You must be sensible about it. You gave her a happy life and fine children, and I'm sure she's happy where she is."

Meanwhile, the women, gathered in the kitchen, which was always rather a dark place, were drinking coffee and eating cake.

When I went to school and began to learn the history of the Gauls, I nicknamed my grandfather Vercingetorix because of his big drooping mustache, which must once have been red, but which I only remember as white.

I recall other funerals, not at home, but among our relations, with my mother wearing a crepe veil over her face, and my father usually in black, unless he was in his working clothes.

The most important incident concerned the old house and the new one. My grandfather had built, on the empty plot that joined and continued our courtyard, a house facing Rue du Four, parallel to Rue Bourgeoise.

Because it was his profession, he must have built it with love, putting stained glass in the staircase windows, ceramic trim on the brick façade, and pink tiles alternating with almost black ones on the roof.

I tend to get dates confused. I should be able to remember them; my sister, Louise, must be able to say on what date such and such an aunt married, the ages of her children, when some cousin died.

I wonder if it was, and still is, through indifference on my part, or if, even as a child, I watched it all without feeling that I belonged to it.

I did not, on the other hand, feel alien to it. I was never the kind of boy who rebels against family life or against his milieu. I accepted its rites, I accepted those of my neighborhood, where I played in the street with my friends, some of whose names and faces—such as Popet's—I can still remember.

I played marbles, I rolled hoops, I whipped tops; later on, I was for a short time on the school soccer team. I was not unsociable.

"You're teasing your sister, Félix!"

Apparently I behaved unkindly toward her. I was jealous of her and deliberately rough. On such occasions, I was sent into the yard, which was full of ladders, sacks, and building materials, or into the street, where the scaffolding was still up.

The story of the two houses was a complicated and somewhat mysterious one; it was only mentioned in whispers in front of my sister and me. My grandmother died at about the time the new house was completed. My

71

grandfather at first stayed on with us in the old one, while my aunt Julie, married to a man named Cassegrain, who owned two trucks and who became a large-scale trucker, settled in the new one.

Cassegrain was a rake, they said. He was loud-mouthed and given to drink, and would admit nobody's superiority. He was a fool, endowed with incredible vitality, and could not endure opposition. Was it true that one day he came across the yard and, finding my mother alone, tried to take advantage of the opportunity?

For weeks, there was whispering at night, after my sister and I had gone to bed, and occasional raised voices.

"Poor Julie! To be saddled with a man like that! And she has such lovely children. . . ."

She had two at the time, one of them a baby, who spent all day in a carriage, which was moved around to catch the sun. All communication between the two houses ceased. Other incidents must have occurred, because the courtyard was subsequently divided in two, first with a wooden fence, painted green, and then with a wall.

I don't know exactly how old my grandfather was when he decided to divide his property between his son and his daughters. My father inherited the business, under certain conditions, and undertook to look after the old man to the end of his days.

I picture all this as though it were a landscape reflected, with distortions, in the waters of a pond. At what point did Aunt Léonore, the only unmarried member of the family, go off one night, leaving a letter to say she was not coming back? I never saw her again. I heard that she was living in Marseille, then Algiers.

As for Vercingetorix, he found it very boring in our

home, with a skinny daughter-in-law who played the piano and cooked his food in an unfamiliar way.

The question was debated at a familly gathering, and eventually Grandfather went over to the other side of the wall to live with his daughter, Julie, in the new house.

Considering what had happened with Cassegrain, this was an act of treachery. The family was split into two camps.

I was in school by then. I was one of the three best pupils in my class, which seemed as natural to me as it did to my parents. My chief rival for first place was Godard, who later became an engineer in the Water Department, and must by now be a municipal councillor of Puteaux, if not, indeed, mayor.

Was it on my teacher's advice that I was sent to the Lycée Pasteur? I used to read a great deal, as yesterday's and today's rain reminded me. When it rained, when it was cold, and we were all shut up in the same room, I used to thrust fingers in my ears in order not to be disturbed in my reading.

I had violin lessons from my other grandfather, Justin Périnel, who had bushy hair, flushed cheekbones, and a feverish look in his eyes. He was poorer than we were, and taught his pupils in a parlor that was so heavily upholstered and so cluttered with knickknacks and ornaments that I always felt stifled there.

He died of tuberculosis. Vercingetorix declared that the same fate awaited my mother, who, however, lived until the end of the Second World War.

"What do you want to be when you grow up?"

I answered categorically:

"A teacher."

"A teacher of what?"

"I don't know."

My examining magistrate, a sensitive man, who tried a little too hard to understand, maybe, asked me a number of questions about my childhood, precisely because, I imagine, he suspected my case was less simple than it seemed.

He did not try to hide his sympathy or his curiosity, in spite of our respective situations. One day, after a fairly long interrogation on facts, he asked me:

"What was your ambition when you were young?"

"To become a teacher."

He did not ask of what, but why. I had never thought about that. I had assumed it to be quite natural. Besides, I had originally dreamed of becoming a bus conductor. I told him this. And when he spoke to me afterward, with a thoughtful air, I guessed which psychology textbooks he had been reading.

"Don't you find it odd? A teacher is *in* the class, but not part of it. I mean he's not one of the rank and file; he doesn't belong to the group."

"It never occurred to me," I said apologetically.

He added, with a laugh:

"Many boys want to become bus conductors or policemen, because of the uniform. In your case, I think I discern a point in common with the teaching profession. The conductor is *in* the bus but he, too, belongs in a different category from the passengers around him. . . ."

I'll leave these arguments to other people. For a long time now, I have given up trying to learn about life or myself through books.

Latin was not my own choice originally. My mother would have liked me to be a doctor. She lived in terror of the scaffolding, the soaring walls, the planks stretched

74

across the void, along which my father walked like a circus acrobat when he was supervising men at work on a building.

There had been six or seven workmen in my grand-father's day, but soon we had twenty of them, sometimes thirty at busy periods. Father spent less and less time in his working clothes, and more and more sitting in his little office, amid a growing heap of green files, with his jacket off, his shirt sleeves turned up, and his tie loosened.

My sister was taking piano lessons and used to practice several hours a day. The sound is a familiar one to me, like the noise of our first van, which had to be started with the aid of a crank and was often stubborn.

Shortly afterward a small truck replaced the handcarts.

When I had to choose, I opted for Latin and Greek. Was this because the teacher had stressed the difficulties of Greek? Many are called, he had said, but few are chosen, implying that Greek was the supreme attain-ment; I was also attracted by the mysterious quality of the writing.

My examining magistrate might perhaps maintain that this was yet another attempt of mine to escape from life— from the life of the group, of course. Greek classes were the most sparsely populated, and among the senior boys who were preparing to take the *bachot*, there were only six or seven studying Greek. You saw them in the court-yard chatting with the teacher on an equal footing.

My grandfather Allard died while I was in my second or third year. He had been increasingly dissatisfied lately with life with the Cassegrains, despite his affection for his daughter, Julie. The house was noisy, his son-in-law was insolent and vulgar, and he came more and more frequently to take refuge with us.

75

He died in the courtyard, on the other side of the wall, sitting in his chair. His pipe had dropped from his hands. They spoke of heart disease. I took so little part in family life that I don't know much about it. When I was not studying, I was reading. I often read a book a day, sometimes two or even three during holidays.

I watched my sister grow into a young girl with some astonishment, and I was surprised by the way she talked about boys. From the sexual point of view, I was not precocious, and it was in the company of a schoolmate, Ledoux, more enterprising than I, that, at fifteen, I made my first approach to a woman, a professional we'd had our eyes on for several days.

"Both of you?" she had exclaimed.

Our naïveté amused her. Afterward, as though by mutual agreement, Ledoux and I avoided one another.

In 1930—I'm almost sure of the date—we spent a month at the seashore. My father drove us to Dieppe, where he had rented a floor in a villa. He had to leave us—my mother, my sister, and me—after a few days, because summer was always his busiest time.

I hear the rain falling, I smell the odor of the dog and of my drying overcoat, and my own skin, since the stove gives out considerable heat. Like the one we had in Puteaux, you can never set it at just the temperature you want.

I have other memories I might recall. What I would find interesting would be to compare them with those that Philippe and Daniel will have someday of the same period in their lives. Don't people say it is that period that matters most, and on it the rest of our lives depends?

For my part, I cannot recognize myself in the schoolboy

I once was—perhaps because I did not try to live my own life, but buried myself deeper and deeper in books.

I remember one evening seeing my father—a powerfully built man, with a ruddier complexion than the rest of us—come back from one of his building sites with plaster dust in his hair and on his shoulders. It must have been wintertime, since I was not working in my bedroom, but in the parlor, where there was a fire.

I was preparing a Greek composition, and he bent over the page I was covering with the signs he found so mysterious. He stood behind me, and I could not see him. Yet I was conscious of his satisfaction and pride, of a sort of respect suddenly felt by him for his son.

My childhood was not an unhappy one; nor was it dreary or disturbed. I have as many sunny memories as cloudy ones: in the courtyard, for instance, on a chair tipped back, with my feet on a pile of planks and a book in my hand, and all the noises of the house and those of Puteaux and the tugs on the Seine running through my brain, to be recorded there without my knowledge.

IT IS THREE O'CLOCK, and it's still raining. My overcoat, which dries slowly, weighs twice as much as usual, and, since I have no other, there is no question of going out again. I think, moreover, that another walk through puddles would scarcely appeal to Bib.

Some time ago, on a Saturday evening when I carried the daily receipts to the mezzanine floor, Madame Annelet asked me:

"What do you do on Sundays, Félix?"

"Nothing," I replied simply.

She looked at me insistently, and I concluded that she had understood. She does nothing either. She does nothing all week but read magazines and historical novels. Since she has become almost tied to her room, I have the feeling every Saturday evening that she's going to call me back.

On Sunday mornings, she still has Renée. But the girl leaves immediately after lunch. That's her free afternoon and evening; she has another evening during the week. There is nobody on the ground floor, where the shutter remains closed. Madame Annelet can't ring for me. A cold supper is placed by her side. On a day like today, except for the patter of rain and the noise of passing buses, absolute silence must reign.

For some time now, my walks with Bib have been curtailed on account of my health. As recently as two years ago, we used to walk along the quays as far as Charenton, looking at the barrels behind the railings at Bercy and the canal boats moored one behind the other, and pausing beside the occasional fisherman.

We know all the benches well. And I also know all the café terraces, where I pause as soon as the sun breaks through a little, and sometimes order a glass of white wine, which never tastes the same as that I drank when I got out of Central Prison.

I am amazed whenever I have to consider dates. I am now forty-eight. More precisely, I shall be forty-nine in January. Most men my age are better preserved than I am; I'm prematurely old.

This has no connection with the rather vague question I'm asking myself: How have I spent my life—how has my time passed during those thirty years since my *bachot* and my time at the Sorbonne?

On the one hand, I cannot recognize myself in the young man I then was, and, on the other, I feel as if it were yesterday. I am sometimes shocked by the idea that a life can produce so little, can pass almost without leaving any trace.

At eighteen, or twenty, when I was still given to daydreaming, I constructed a little personal theory, which was neither scientific nor philosophical, but which fascinated me.

From a physics lesson, I gathered that a certain exchange takes place between bodies that come into contact with one another; that friction, for instance, leaves its mark on objects.

So I imagined that we leave our mark on the places through which we pass during our lives, somewhat the way game leaves a trail, which dogs recognize by sniffing the air. But not a smell—a different sort of trail, or, rather, a succession of ghosts, drifts of ectoplasm.

I discovered long ago that nothing of the sort happens, that the only images of us that survive—and for how short a time!—are the distorted images, often caricatures, floating in the memories of those who have known us.

It is not for this reason that I dog the footsteps of Philippe and Daniel; the proof being that I never show myself to them. The last time they saw me, they were less than six years old, and I was still a fine-looking man, well dressed and not overweight.

All that I'm doing is watching them grow up and convincing myself that they are turning into men. At their age, hadn't I, too, begun to think I was a man?

My going to the university caused no family arguments. Since I had embarked on the study of classical languages, it was obviously the only course to take. My father was rather sorry that his only son would not eventually carry on his business, but in his heart he was proud of me.

I took him, late one afternoon, to Rue des Ecoles, and he walked respectfully on the ancient stones of the courtyard.

"Why, they've put up a statue to Victor Hugo!"

Nothing could have touched him more, Hugo being one of the few authors familiar to him. Seeing Pasteur at the other end of the steps reassured him still further, as if, between two such men, I was in good hands.

I showed him the lecture rooms, whose names he read on the pediments: Turgot, Richelieu, Guizot . . . He sat down for a moment on one of the seats in a room where we were alone. Nonetheless, he lowered his voice as if in church.

I might have become a professor. This career, on which I had decided at an age when I didn't really understand the meaning of the term, would probably have suited me.

At Santé Prison, where I stayed during the preliminary investigation of my case, I was asked to give elementary lessons to some young delinquents. I agreed. For reasons unknown to me—lack of space, no doubt—I was soon transferred to Fresnes, where I stayed only a few weeks and where my only occupation was arguing with my lawyer, Maître Forniol.

Once I had been sentenced to five years at hard labor, I was taken to Melun, where, theoretically, I should have undergone six months of solitary confinement. Such are the administrative regulations. You live alone in a cell, day and night, seeing nobody except, once a day, the chief guard and, once a month, the director or his assistant. Silence is obligatory.

For longer sentences than mine, the period of solitary confinement is a whole year, and I've heard it described by most prisoners as a nightmare.

The prison doctor, who looked in from time to time, was surprised not to find me depressed, and indeed seemed worried by my indifference. As I learned later, he went so far as to recommend that a special watch be kept on me, in case I tried to commit suicide.

"I got the impression that you're not reacting," he told me one day. "Do you sleep normally? Don't you sometimes get a choking feeling?"

"No."

"Are you eating all right?"

"Whatever I'm given."

"Have you had any visitors from outside?"

"No."

"Or any letters?"

"None."

He wanted to make me tell him everything, to see in what tone I spoke, although he knew all about me from my record, in which all such things were put down.

"No discomfort? No pain anywhere?"

"No."

I had been given a choice among various manual tasks and, for lack of a proper vocation, I had chosen to cut out puppets.

"Do you get your daily walk?"

In the yard. It was compulsory. You saw nothing but walls and bricks. As you walked, you heard, like an echo, the footsteps of other men walking in other parts of the star-shaped yard. There was nobody to be seen but the guard in the center, gloomy, indifferent, doing his job.

"If I were you, I'd ask to be seen by the neurologist.

You're entitled to it. I can't force you; but it would at least allow you to spend a few days under observation in the infirmary."

"My nerves are perfectly sound."

I had no desire to be questioned by a specialist. I had been asked so many questions during the last six months, and had been watched as if I presented some problem.

The director had taken an interest in me, too; like the doctor, he was baffled by my total lack of reaction. His interest was due, no doubt, to the fact that prisoners from a certain social class usually complain, demand special treatment, fall ill or pretend to.

For hundreds of years, monks have chosen a way of life not unlike this. And how many city dwellers deliberately choose an even stricter routine than that of a prison?

"I don't think you'll be kept long in a cell, Allard. In my last report, I suggested curtailing your period of solitary confinement, and I stressed your good conduct."

What good conduct? Had they expected me to hit the chief guard during his daily visit?

"According to your file, you've taken some advanced literary studies. Would you like to be attached to the library? The man who's been our librarian for six years is due to be released next week. The post is a responsible one. It involves, not merely distributing books here and there, but guiding readers, particularly young prisoners."

I did the job for nearly four years. It was rather like being a teacher, after all, and I recognized the same smell of old paper as in the Bibliothèque Sainte-Geneviève. Almost all my fellow prisoners had visitors. I expected none. And I never had a single one. I did not mind. Far from it!

I followed a monotonous schedule, just as I do today in my somewhat larger prison, which includes Rue des Arquebusiers, a little of Boulevard Beaumarchais, Place des Vosges, and the quays along the Seine.

I still follow rules, which I have laid down for myself or which have been laid down for me, and I remain confined within invisible walls.

Last Sunday, I allowed myself to interrupt my schedule by going for lunch to Place du Tertre, and, as far as I can judge, it did not suit me.

It's strange, surely, that my recollections of the Sorbonne convey the same impression of routine. I was apparently as free as possible, since I was past the stage when my parents could regulate my life. They knew nothing about the time of my classes, the work I was doing, or the complicated setup of various examinations for diplomas.

They trusted me, they felt no anxiety about me. They were chiefly concerned about my sister, who had begun to lead her own life and assume an independent air.

"If only she could find some steady young man who'd help me and take over the business someday!" my father would say with a sigh.

I entered the Sorbonne in 1932. I was a tall, lanky adolescent, and nobody could have foretold that I would eventually become a mass of unhealthy fat, on whom any garment looks shapeless.

I still had my room in the old house, and the shelves were crammed with books, as in my present room.

At the Lycée Pasteur I had been an outstanding pupil, and my teachers were confident of my success. What happened to me during the following spring, that of 1933?

I am incapable of answering that. I had chosen the compulsory subjects for candidates for the teaching profession, and had drawn up my program.

At first I was passionately interested in philosophy, and all winter I kept up my Greek, as well as studying ancient and medieval history.

The streetcar still ran in those days, and I used to take it early in the morning, with my books tucked under my arm, and read on the way.

I took notes at lectures, and usually had lunch in some cheap restaurant before going to my next class.

When the weather improved and the days grew longer, I got into the habit of sitting on an open café terrace or in the Luxembourg Garden, and not returning to Puteaux before nightfall.

I went around in a daze. I became absorbed into the spring, the light, the warmth, the coming and going of the crowd. I watched passers-by and followed them with my thoughts as though to reconstitute their life stories.

I suppose that was the nearest I ever came to what is called "happiness." The outside world permeated my skin: shadow and sunlight, the trees in the squares, the continuous movement along Boulevard Saint-Michel, as well as the smell of beer and the click of billiard balls.

For two whole months, I read my books absent-mindedly, my eye soon distracted by the sight of a beggar, a red or a white dress, a child's boat sailing on the water of the pond. I could have spent an hour without being bored watching anything living—an ant, a bee, a flower.

I had been trained in the discipline of the lycée, and now I was let loose in a world of movement and color in which I could enjoy myself without having to account to anyone.

I failed, by one point, my French literature exam, although the subject was an easy one: the theater during the first half of the eighteenth century. I did not tell them at home. I had just made the acquaintance of a red-haired girl who worked as a maid for a doctor in Faubourg Saint-Germain. I had to wait in the evening on the edge of her metal bed on the seventh floor, until her employers had finished dinner and she had done the dishes.

On her account, I spent only one week in Dieppe with my mother and sister, pretending that I had some indispensable work to do in Paris. Ironically, I quarreled with the girl a few days later. It took me a couple of weeks to find somebody else, and I spent that time tramping through deserted summer streets.

The whole of this period is bathed, in my memory, in a kind of luminous haze. Nothing mattered. Nothing was important. I would leap at random onto the platform of a bus, to go wherever it took me. I would stare into shop windows, sit down in cafés. If I mentioned billiards earlier, it's because I played the game for two or three months, on the second floor of the Brasserie Cluny.

My parents' chief source of worry was still my sister. They treated me as a grown man and had no doubts about my future.

Yet, by the end of the second winter, I was aiming only to get the bachelor of arts degree, and thus had given up all thoughts of the teaching profession.

I was not unduly alarmed, though I did sometimes have a moment of panic when I thought about it.

"What are you going to do later?"

I'd heard that question so often! Well, between the ages of nineteen and twenty and a half, I never put it to myself. I deliberately ignored it. I chose subjects as the fancy took me, and thus signed up for a course in sociology, to which I went only three times, and I nearly took up Chinese. The Sorbonne was merely an excuse, a background, a way of life.

For years we had had no servant in the house. My grandmother had never had one; nor had my aunts, so far as I knew. It was less a question of money than a moral attitude: a woman must run her own house and prepare the meals.

My grandfather had built suburban villas in the traditional craftsman's way, brick by brick. My father, right from the start, had equipped himself for building with reinforced concrete, and when he got an order for a six-story building, he increased his materials and rented some land just outside Puteaux.

These changes must have coincided more or less with my parents' hiring of a maid and their purchase of a new car—no longer a van, but a real car, with four doors. Inevitably, I demanded to learn to drive and take the test. Once I got my license, I borrowed the car more and more frequently.

I had companions, but no friends. I went with girls, but never long with the same one. In spite of the car, I didn't act the rich man's son. I had little pocket money, and although I like being well dressed, I did not attach too much importance to it.

As I write, trying to isolate this three-year period, I feel increasingly amazed at my own lack of awareness. I ought to have realized that sooner or later I would have to tell my parents that I had managed to secure only two diplomas, one in medieval history and the other in the general history of philosophy. These led nowhere, opened no professional doors. Teaching was now out of the question, and I had learned nothing else.

I had read. I had read almost everything that matters. I had discussed things for hours, sitting in the smoke-filled room of the Café d'Harcourt or outside on the terrace. I had argued for hours about Russian, English, and American writers, about the lives of great men, about evolution, and I don't know what all.

And other times? I lived for the moment, taking my fill of selfish and fleeting pleasures.

The streets fascinated me, but I could also sit still in a square, my eyes half closed, enjoying the sun's warmth on my cyclids and feeling perfectly happy.

At eighteen, my sister became engaged to a salesman named Noblet, and I believe my parents heaved a great sigh of relief at the thought that they would soon be rid of their responsibility.

I don't know where or how the couple met, which proves how much I had lost contact with my family. I merely remember the wedding and the small apartment they went to live in, in Rue Lamarck, in Montmartre.

I don't know, either, if my father tried to persuade Noblet to go into his business. The fact remains that a few years later the latter bought a hardware business in Rouen—why Rouen, I wonder—where he now owns the town's biggest household-goods store.

They have four children. I have seen only the two oldest, both as dark-haired as their father but with the blue eyes of the Allards, as they say in my family.

I still had to do my military service, from which, as a student, I had been granted a postponement. And I also had to earn my living.

Meanwhile, I was quite happy just to breathe in life, as, when I was a small child, apparently I used to breathe the smell of an orange for hours and burst into tears when anyone attempted to peel it.

THE YELLOW NOTEBOOK

Monday, November 18

9 P.M.

YESTERDAY I HAD TO CRAMP MY WRITING, because I had reached the end of my notebook and had no other. Today I went to buy one at the stationery store, and I chose a yellow one for a change. I am rather worried at having written so much without realizing it. It won't do for this to become a mania, and for notebooks to accumulate. And I don't like my complacency, the pleasure I seem to take in talking about myself. When I bought the yellow notebook, I vowed that there won't be any others, that this will be the last, that under no circumstances will this self-assessment I have undertaken become an excuse.

It has stopped raining. During the night, the wind began to blow violently, and Bib and I, living under the roof as we do, got the full strength of it.

This morning it was blowing like a gale. The papers talk of ships in difficulties in the Channel, of havoc wrought on the Atlantic seaboard, of a factory chimney collapsing somewhere in Normandy, and of trains held up by trees and electricity poles lying across the rails.

In our district, a number of roof tiles have been blown off and lie shattered in the street, and from time to time a few more come down. I am always excited by seeing the forces of Nature let loose; on other days, I seldom glance out of the bookshop window, but today I turned to look out at the street dozens of times.

It was fascinating to observe the attitudes of people outside. Those going toward the Bastille leaned backward, with their coats blown tight against their shoulders as the wind drove them on, whereas those going toward the Place de la République bent forward. Several times I saw a man running after his hat, bending with outstretched hand to pick it up just as it went racing off again.

We had few customers. I expected this, and so did Madame Annelet, who feels nervous and ill at ease when the wind blows. She kept sending for me. Renée looked as if she hadn't slept, which reminded me of the little redhead on Boulevard Saint-Germain. I wonder what became of her. I ask myself that about everyone, male or female, who has ever crossed, or come into contact with, my life.

If they feel the same curiosity about me, what sort of fate do they ascribe to me?

At exactly seven minutes past eleven—I looked at the time on the electric clock that hangs above the flowered curtain—the telephone rang. I picked up the receiver and said hello.

"Annelet's bookshop?"

"Yes."

A woman's voice, which I did not recognize. Some of our customers give their orders by telephone, though not many of them.

After a slight hesitation, it seemed to me, the voice went on:

"Who is this?"

"The assistant."

This time the hesitation was so unmistakable that I, in my turn, asked:

"Did you wish to speak to Madame Annelet?"

She has a telephone beside her bed. The two instruments are connected to the same line, so she can listen to all conversations, which she unfailingly does, as I presently found out.

"You are Monsieur Allard?"

Since I left Melun, nobody has called me, except the few customers I have mentioned, who know me as Monsieur Félix. I said yes, with some reluctance.

"Félix Allard?" the voice insisted.

"Yes."

Another pause. We had not been cut off, however, since I could still hear the sound of breathing. At last a click told me the other receiver had been replaced.

Madame Annelet allowed time for me to get over my surprise, ask myself questions, and construct hypotheses. I am convinced that she must have exercised great self-control not to ring for me immediately. She waited five minutes before pressing the bell. I went up. Renée was cleaning the room. The vacuum stood on the carpet.

"Do you know who that was, Félix?"

I have, at long last, grown used to being looked at like that, with those unmoving eyes that miss no trace of agitation or untruthfulness, no inner movement however vague and fleeting. One feels naked, or as though surprised in some humiliating posture, in the bathroom, for instance. My sister had the habit of suddenly opening the door when I was on the toilet. It never worried her to be seen thus.

"No. I have no idea."

"You didn't recognize the voice?"

"I tried to. I'm still trying . . . without success."

"It wasn't your wife's?"

"Certainly not. My wife's voice is high-pitched."

"She might have disguised it on purpose."

"Not to that extent."

Nor was it the voice of Monique—Daniel's mother—who lives a little way down Boulevard Beaumarchais.

"Have you picked up anybody lately?"

"No. I have not been near a woman for three months. I have not wanted to."

"Somebody who knows you may have seen you coming in here or going out, or caught sight of you through the window."

"It's possible."

"Are you frightened?"

"Of what?"

I was disturbed and uneasy nonetheless, and I still am. She went on after lighting a cigarette:

"It must be somebody who knew you long ago, and, since you've changed, isn't sure that it's really you. It's highly probable that you will soon meet this woman, or that she will write to you."

One of the few customers we had that day came in at that moment, and I went down to the shop to serve him. I did not go upstairs again until shortly before lunchtime.

"Tell me, Félix . . . There's something I've been wanting to ask you ever since you spoke of your intention."

"What intention?"

I was at a loss. I felt as remote as I used to feel when sitting on a chair in the Luxembourg Garden.

"Of going away for good. You must have thought about how you'll do it, surely?"

In the first place, I had never taken her into my con-

94

fidence. I hadn't told her about anything; it was she who had wormed it out of me. In any case, I resented her assumption.

"Do you own a gun?"

I smiled. She, however, remained quite serious, as though it was a matter of concern to her.

"Poison? Have you got hold of poison?"

This was as indecent as my sister's bursting into the bathroom. I'm beginning to believe that women lack our sense of propriety. I remained evasive.

"It depends on what you call poison."

"Sleeping tablets?"

"Perhaps."

"You have definitely decided? Aren't you afraid of changing your mind and wanting to go on living once it's too late? That must be appalling! Not to be able to move or to call out, to lie there motionless waiting, without knowing exactly how long it'll take . . . Go and eat, Félix! . . . You've spoiled lunch for me. . . ."

I ate mine at Chez Rose, the little restaurant opposite where I live, among packers and truck drivers. They are used to me and to Bib. He knows them, and goes up to sniff at them one after the other, wagging his stump of a tail.

Afterward we cut short our walk, because the wind took my breath away, and my lips must have been blue.

During the afternoon there were no telephone calls. Madame Annelet did not mention the morning call and made no new references to my death.

I was thinking, not of my own death, but, reverting to what I wrote yesterday, of another death, which changed my destiny overnight.

It was the seventh of June, one of the few dates I'm

95

quite sure of. A strong, scorching midsummer sun slowed traffic in the streets so much that even the buses seemed to crawl. Colors were darker and denser, and the foliage of the trees along Boulevard Saint-Michel was as still and dull as in a stage set.

At half past ten I was sitting outside a café, the d'Harcourt, in a yellow cane chair, in front of a glass of beer. A dark young woman was sitting less than a yard away from me at another small table, and had just eaten two croissants, dipping them into her *café crème*.

We glanced at one another a few times, intermittently—what I used to call question-mark glances. It was a game I enjoyed playing. It either works or it doesn't.

It worked. After a few moments, she could not restrain her laughter.

"You *are* funny. What do you want from me?"

"I don't know yet."

She had a slight foreign accent. A little later, I learned from her that her name was Sonia, that her father was a Russian engineer working in Belgium, where she was born.

I had the car. Toward noon, we got out of it, Sonia and I, in front of an inn on the banks of the Seine, a few kilometers from Corbeil. We had lunch outside. When our coffee was brought, I went inside to whisper to the landlady, who handed me a key. By two o'clock, Sonia was lying naked on a iron bed, in a whitewashed room, with closed shutters, that smelled of slightly musty hay.

"Have you got a girl?"

"No."

"You'd rather take advantage of what comes your way, like this? Have you often come to this room?"

"Only once."

It was true.

"Admit that you like change."

"It depends."

We got dressed about five o'clock, after dozing for a while. She was thirsty, so we went back to the terrace and drank a bottle of white wine—Samur, I remember. I was weary, enervated. She insisted, nevertheless, on my stopping by a wood so she could pick some broom. All those complex and rather sickly smells: her sweat, the broom, the white wine, the hay in the mattress . . .

I dropped her at six o'clock on the corner of Boulevard Raspail, and in the rear-view mirror I saw her in the middle of the sidewalk renewing her powder and lipstick, while men turned around to look at her.

I drove back to Puteaux. Leaving the car in the yard, I pushed open the front door, calling out as usual:

"When do we eat?"

I fell silent immediately. I saw in front of me the staircase leading to the second floor, on my left the kitchen door, which should have been open, and on the right the parlor door. I don't know why, but everything looked empty, frozen into stillness. Then, slowly and almost solemnly, the left-hand door opened, and I saw my mother standing motionless for a moment. Then she flung herself into my arms and burst into sobs.

Over her shoulder I caught sight, in the kitchen, of people I had not expected to see there: my sister and her husband, Aunt Julie, who had not set foot in our house for several years, Victor the foreman, an old woman from the neighborhood, and various other people, sitting or standing motionless, with expressionless faces.

"Your father, Félix! . . . Oh, God! Who'd have thought this morning . . . He was so cheerful! . . ."

It was the first time I had held my mother in my arms this way, not like a son, but as though I had suddenly taken my father's place.

"You know what he was like. . . . He wanted to see everything for himself. . . . He was up there on the fifth floor, on a plank that . . . Come in here!"

Carefully and noiselessly, she turned the handle of the parlor door. She pushed it open just as softly, and in the half-darkness I saw my father, dead, already wrapped in his shroud, his hands clasped over a chaplet, an unlighted candle on either side of the bed, which had been brought down from his room.

She whispered in my ear:

"Go and kiss him. . . ."

I think she must have given me a slight push. I took three or four steps, bent forward, and laid my lips, furtively and without pressure, on the cold forehead.

Afterward, I don't quite know what happened. I rushed off. I hurried upstairs, flung myself full length on my bed, and tried to cry, without success. My chest ached. I chewed the bedcover.

Why should it be that day, of all days, while I had been . . .

I muttered between my teeth:

"It's my fault. . . . It's my fault. . . . It's because of me that it happened. . . ."

Not just because of Sonia, the inn, and that hateful broom. But because of everything. Because of my deceitfulness, those three years I had stolen from everybody.

I thumped the bed with my fist.

"No, no. I won't . . ."

Someone touched my shoulder, and I turned around furiously.

"What . . ."

It was my sister.

"Calm down, Félix. You've got to keep calm for Mother's sake. She's had a terrible time. . . . She's been very brave. Don't deprive her of the little strength she has left. . . ."

What right had Louise to talk to me like that? She was no longer one of the family. She had another name. She didn't live with us.

"You'd better come down. Mother's getting worried."

"What are all those people doing downstairs?"

"There's old Madame Rinquet, who laid him out when they brought him back from the hospital. . . . Mother was beside herself. . . ."

"Wasn't he . . . ?"

It was hard to say the word.

"Wasn't he killed immediately?"

Why was she suddenly embarrassed?

"Yes, probably . . . We don't know. . . . Victor was in the building yard. . . . The local doctor wasn't home, and Victor thought it best to tell the police, who sent an ambulance. . . ."

I looked at her spitefully.

"And then?"

"Well, nothing . . . When he got to the hospital, it was too late, and they sent him back to us here."

"What time did the accident happen?"

"About half past ten . . . By twelve o'clock they'd brought him back. . . . Mother called me. . . . I hurried over with André. He tried to reach you; he called the secretary's office at the Sorbonne. . . ."

I reddened in sudden panic, wondering what André had been told.

"They couldn't find you. . . . Nobody knew where you were. . . ."

But I knew. When my father lay dying, I was drinking beer in a café on Boulevard Saint-Michel and ogling my neighbor with stupid smiles.

While he was being brought home, we were speeding toward the inn on the banks of the Seine, and while the parlor was being turned into a mortuary chamber, I was making love.

My hands still smelled of that girl and that broom. I went to wash them. I would have liked to take a bath, to purify myself. I considered myself shameful.

"What are you going to do?"

"I'm going down."

"That's not what I mean. I'm talking about the future, about Mother, about the house . . ."

She'd thought of everything, of course! But I remember chiefly the way my widowed mother had quite naturally flung herself into my arms. I was as tall as my father, but not quite as broad or as tough. Nonetheless, I was now the man of the family.

"Come on. Come downstairs first. . . ."

And as I dried my hands, I stared into the mirror at my tense face and questioning eyes.

IT WAS THE YEAR of the Popular Front. I am sure of that because the funeral procession met a demonstration carrying red flags, slogans, banners waving over people's heads, and the demonstrators almost all took off their caps as they passed. I also recall seeing, on the walls, posters depicting a clenched fist.

I cannot remember what pretext my sister found for

spending the night in our house with her husband. She may have been afraid that this first evening would be too painful for my mother. As it happened, late that afternoon Dr. Chollet, who had looked after us from birth, dropped in to see Mother and gave her a sedative.

Consequently, I had to dine with Louise and my brother-in-law and then sit with them for some time. I discovered then to what extent I had become a stranger. During the past year, I had scarcely come home except to sleep, and I could easily count the number of meals I had eaten with my family.

Details that ought to have been familiar to me surprised me. I hardly knew the maid, an Alsatian girl named Frida. She, too, now that my father was dead, began to treat me as the head of the house, and she did not pay the same respect to Louise's husband, in her eyes a mere son-in-law.

"Have you reached any decision, Félix?" Louise asked.

I stubbornly refused to follow her onto that ground or discuss anything with her.

"I've got to know. If the business is going to be sold, I suppose Mother will come to live with us."

Did she have an ulterior motive? I'd rather not commit myself about that. I stayed with them for another half hour out of politeness, and then pretended to have a headache in order to go to bed.

They must have left early the next morning. That has gone from my memory. But I have a clear recollection of the house, with its shutters almost all closed, because of the sunlight, and the whisper of the sultry air outside.

We ate alone together for the first time, my mother and I, and as I looked at her I calculated her age. My father had been fifty-one; he was four years older than her; so she must be forty-seven, which seemed old to me. I had been surprised, those last three days, to hear people say, more than once:

"To be taken so young!"

To my mind, my father had had a full life and enjoyed his fair share.

I can't attempt to reconstruct our comings and goings that day. I know only that during the afternoon, when I came down from my bedroom, I found my mother in the office, a small, partially glassed-in room in which we seldom set foot.

I had looked for her everywhere else, and I was surprised to find her absorbed in reading letters, particularly because she was wearing her glasses, which I had seldom seen. They had recently been prescribed for her for reading and writing.

"Am I disturbing you?" I asked rather awkwardly.

She smiled at me with that new smile, which she kept to the end of her days, a bittersweet smile that irritated me more than once, particularly after a few years. I don't know why it reminded me of the color mauve, which, when I was small, women wore for half-mourning.

"You know you never disturb me."

"What are you looking for?"

"Victor needs a letter that must have come quite recently."

"Would you like me to help you?"

Then, suddenly, just as she was looking at me, I made my decision.

"You know, Mother, you can count on me."

"What do you mean?"

"That I'm going to stay. I'll try to learn the ropes."

"You're going to carry on your father's business?"

"Why not?"

"And you'd sacrifice your career, your studies, all the trouble you've been to?"

We were cheating, both of us. She was pretending to be surprised at my decision, although she expected it from me. I, for my part, had no alternative.

"I don't care all that much about becoming a teacher."

"Can you see yourself climbing up scaffolding?"

"Maybe it's not really necessary for me to do that. I'll have people to help me, including Victor. He'll gradually tell me what I have to know."

"You're doing it for my sake, aren't you?"

"No, no!"

That was to be the tone of our relationship for the next ten years. She kissed me effusively, but this time she did not cling to me.

"You're quite sure, Félix? You won't regret it someday?"

"Tomorrow I'll start work with Victor."

His name was Victor Michou, and he was about my father's age. He was almost as broad as he was tall, with the neck and shoulders and biceps of a wrestler. He took considerable pride in having traveled all around France as journeyman, going from town to town, from one province to another, often on foot, to learn his trade and eventually to become master of it.

He was married to a woman who was even tinier than my mother, and their only sorrow was that they had no children.

"You'll see, Monsieur Félix! For an educated man like

you, it won't be hard. I left school at twelve myself, and it took years to get some things into this head of mine. . . ."

In my father's time, an accountant, Monsieur Beauchef, used to come one afternoon a week to go over the books. I got him to devote a whole day to us, then two, and he ended up working exclusively for us.

We went to the lawyer's, and I signed an agreement allowing me five years' respite before paying Louise her share of the inheritance.

This was another panel of my life, of quite a different color from the previous one, and, moreover, very unlike what was to come after.

My mother, to my surprise, not only took an interest in the business, but also was far better informed about it than I had imagined, which makes me suppose that my father must have talked to her about it when they were alone together. Perhaps he even asked her advice on occasion.

She knew the names of customers, suppliers, workmen, and also technical terms, which I had often heard without bothering about their meaning. She knew what stage the various buildings had reached, and had met several of the architects.

I have referred to a bittersweet smile. The word might serve to describe our whole existence. Let's say that it was pleasantly monotonous. We were fond of one another, Mother and I, but I realized that I scarcely knew her, and she probably made the same discovery about me.

"What are you going to do about your military service, now that you're no longer a student?"

"My postponement's valid for a year. After that we'll see."

It was Noblet, my sister's husband, who solved my problem, I'm sorry to admit; I don't like feeling indebted to him. We have never quarreled, but neither have we ever sought closer contact. I dislike seeing an outsider involved with our family concerns.

He knew a deputy or a senator, who secured a further two-year postponement for me, on the grounds of my supporting a widowed mother.

Contrary to what might have been supposed, I adapted myself very well to my trade. Thanks to Victor and Monsieur Beauchef, I soon learned to draw up a building estimate, and the architects were also helpful to me.

Next, Fernand Dinaire, an energetic and intelligent young man, about thirty, with some years' experience, was hired as construction foreman when the business grew.

"Don't you ever think of getting married, Félix? You can't go on as you are for the rest of your life. . . ."

My mother, needless to say, was not really anxious for me to get married. We were almost like a married couple. She soon treated me as she used to treat my father, with the respect that, in certain circles, is still paid to the head of the family.

"Why don't you go out in the evenings more? It would make a change for you. At your age, you ought to be seeing friends, getting to know girls. . . ."

She spoke like that to sound me out. Actually, I used to go out once or twice a week and also usually took my mother to the movies or the theater on Saturday nights.

"Look at that girl in the third row. Don't you think she's pretty? She has such an attractive smile!"

In 1938, we decided together to have the house repainted, outside and inside, the kitchen modernized, the office enlarged, and a second bathroom installed.

"I hardly ever see you with a book. You used to be such a reader!"

It was true. Almost overnight I had lost my taste for reading. I had emerged from my Latin Quarter daze merely to become absorbed in another. I must be incapable of being interested in more than one thing at a time.

I had become a serious businessman, and my age no longer aroused suspicion. I dressed differently. I had grown broader. I walked with a firmer, more masculine step, and I spoke with assurance, sometimes, even on the job, roughly.

I don't think I was playing a part, or that at each period of my life I have assumed the skin of a particular character. I did not imagine myself a building contractor; I *was* one—just as on Boulevard Saint-Michel I had been an authentic student.

After a series of postponements, military service caught up with me. I was sent, in August 1939, to Versailles— this, again, was thanks to my family responsibilities. When war was declared, I had not completed my training, and could scarcely handle a gun.

Three weeks later, as had happened to my father in 1914, I was sent back to Puteaux and put in charge of building air-raid shelters. I was still in uniform, and some of my workmen, who had been dispersed through mobilization, came back to me on special assignment.

When the Germans entered Paris, we merely resumed civilian clothes, and my mother, terrified by the possibility of my being taken off to Germany, patiently burned my military belongings. My helmet and gas mask must still be in the Seine, somewhere below the bridge.

Paris, which the exodus had emptied, gradually filled up again. We got used to rationing, food cards, blackout curtains over the windows, darkened streets, and an oppressive atmosphere. For a time, we felt as if we were outside life.

Frida accomplished miracles to provide a little butter and meat for us. An egg became a luxury. I had the same difficulty in procuring a few sacks of lime or cement.

The wisest course was to pass unnoticed, to withdraw into oneself.

I was not building anything, owing to the lack of materials. Victor and the handful of workmen who had not been sent to Germany could cope with the repairs and alterations we were commissioned to do.

"If your poor father was still here . . ."

Louise's husband was very busy. We scarcely ever saw him or my sister. They were well dressed, well shod, in spite of restrictions, and seemed prosperous. I have good reason to think that it was money earned on the black market that enabled Noblet, after the war, to set up his business in Rouen.

As for the family in the new house, on the other side of the wall, they made no secret of their activities, and when liberation came, they vanished promptly, to avoid trouble. Cassegrain's trucks had kept going as busily as in peacetime, and he'd even bought two new ones.

"Don't you think Julie's wrong to let him do it? I can't help thinking things will end badly one of these days. It was partly your father's and my fault for letting her marry that fellow."

Only once was reference made to Aunt Léonore—on the day of the landings in North Africa.

"I wonder what's going to happen in Algiers, and whether Léonore is still there."

In 1943, I had an affair, which lasted several months, with a girl I met in a shelter during an air raid. She was obviously undernourished. Her eyes were always anxious, even when we were lying side by side in a furnished room on Rue Washington. Her name was Irène, Irène Lautier. Or that was the name she told me. She used to give a start every time she heard steps on the stairs.

"What are you frightened of?"

"I don't know."

"In the street, you always seem to be afraid of being followed, and here of being arrested."

"Hush!"

"And yet you're not Jewish."

"What if I were?"

"You don't look Jewish."

"Would it make any difference to you?"

"None at all."

Before the war, I had never bothered about politics. I did not join any student political group, and I was neither alarmed nor delighted by the Popular Front. Was this also laziness on my part? Or wasn't it simply that mass movements do not interest me?

I felt humiliated at seeing German uniforms in Paris. I only half believed the stories of cruelty toward the Jews, distrusting one sort of propaganda as much as another.

"Listen, Félix, if you don't see me at our rendezvous on Tuesday, take this to the address I'll give you. But *don't* go there before. And don't try to understand."

She took off a tiny silver medal of the Virgin that she wore around her neck.

"Put it into the right hands."

I spent an uncomfortable Sunday because of this. On Tuesday, at the Marbeuf Métro station, I fiddled with the little medal in my pocket. Irène never came. The address was that of a middle-class apartment on Rue de Rennes, fourth floor, left-hand side. The building seemed half empty. Some of the tenants must have taken refuge in the unoccupied zone or in England.

I rang three times, hearing no sound on the other side of the door, and for a moment I suspected a trap. Then the door opened noiselessly, and an elderly man, with dirty gray hair, in a collarless shirt and slippers, looked at me without saying a word.

"Monsieur Demaret?"

"You come from Irène?"

"Yes. She asked me to give you this."

He did not invite me to come in. Through the crack of the door I caught a glimpse of a room with carpets rolled up, furniture covered with dust sheets, and a large livid mirror over the fireplace.

He clenched his teeth as he held out his hand, and didn't even glance at the object. I felt what an effort he made as he muttered:

"Thank you."

Then he shut the door again, and I heard nothing more.

If I am not mistaken, this scene took place in January 1944. Some months later came the Allied landings, the liberation of Paris, and parades down the Champs-Elysées.

There must have been a number of parades. I saw two of them, but I am unable to say whether either was the Victory Parade, as they called it, or the later one with Eisenhower's Americans, which changed the course of my life once more. All I know is that it was the second of the two that did this.

During the first, I was in the crowd at the Rond-Point des Champs-Elysées, squeezed against the *Figaro* building, and I saw almost nothing.

On the eve of the second, Victor said to me:

"If it interests you, I can give you a tip. One of my old friends, whom I still see from time to time, is assistant concierge at the Hotel Claridge. Tell him I sent you, and he'll take you up to the roof. They have a big flat roof with a balustrade around it, from which you can look out over the whole of Paris, and you'll see the parade better than anyone else. . . ."

I went. My mother had thought of going with me, and gave up the idea only at the last minute, from fear of the crowds.

Victor's friend did take me up to the roof, by way of back stairs and passages. The Claridge was packed with uniforms: generals, colonels, and admirals of all the Allied countries, including some Russians—the first I'd seen.

The only civilians there were high-ranking officials, because the hotel had been requisitioned by the government. At every window, on every balcony, champagne and whisky were being drunk; everywhere there were laughing girls, in uniform or in summer dresses.

Why was the roof almost deserted? Probably the hotel guests had not thought of it, or didn't know how to get up there. We must have been less than a dozen all told. Four Americans, with two young women they had certainly not known the day before, had brought up a whole case of champagne. Sitting on the roof with their backs to the Champs-Elysées, they were concerned only with drinking. I noticed one couple, a little way off, embracing.

I looked down at the crowd, the rows of soldiers, the tanks, the guns, the military bands. Airplanes flew back and forth barely twenty yards over my head.

At one point I became aware of a presence on my right. A girl in a navy-blue suit of almost military cut was leaning on the same balustrade, looking down dreamily at the scene below.

How did I come to speak to her? I've forgotten. I must have asked her if she was French, and then if she was attached to the army. She said no, that she was living in the hotel. She was the secretary of a certain Desmarais, with whom she had just returned from London. He was a colonel, and his job must have been an important one to entitle him to a suite at the Claridge.

"And where were you?"

"At home, in Puteaux. . . . Shall we go for a drink?"

We tried in vain to make our way to the bar of the hotel, where somebody spilled a glass of champagne over my trousers.

"Let's go out through the back. It'll be quieter on Rue de Ponthieu."

I had to protect her against indiscreet hands, but failed to prevent five or six men from kissing her avidly. They were almost all in uniform; I was not. I may have felt envious of them.

By contrast, the small bar we went into after crossing the street was a haven of peace.

"What will you have?"

"A Scotch, without ice."

Her name was Anne-Marie Varennes, and I was to marry her three months later.

Wednesday, November 20

10:00 P.M.

I DID NOT WRITE ANYTHING YESTERDAY, and it was not out of laziness, or because I had nothing to say. Ideas and memories are only too plentiful, and I am possessed with a feverish eagerness to unburden myself of them. It's as though I foresaw that I will not get to the end, that something is going to happen that will call everything into question again. I don't know what. I am seized with a kind of uneasiness, an indefinable anguish, and Madame Annelet's gaze is not likely to dispel it. I could swear that she knows, and that she is watching with interest the progress of . . .

Of what? Not of my illness. I speak of that to nobody. I refuse to think of it. I have always hated illness—not because it brings death closer, but because it diminishes us, puts us at the mercy of other people, makes us dependent on them. Even as a boy I was revolted by this idea and hoped that I would die in an accident, like my father, before degeneration set in.

I was serious when I called my employer a witch. Cats have the same air of knowing. I don't believe in clairvoyance, and yet how can her attitude, in our conversation yesterday morning, be ascribed to chance?

The postman comes about half past eight and invariably greets me with "Lovely day!" or else "Terrible weather!"

Yesterday was a lovely day. The wind had veered east and the sun broke through, still pale, but almost joyous. The man laid the letters on the counter and left.

Bills, catalogues, advertisements. Madame Annelet gets few letters. In eight years, not one addressed to me had come to Boulevard Beaumarchais.

Then, yesterday morning, I actually read my own surname and Christian name on an envelope of coarse paper with the local police station's return address. Inside, a printed form had blanks filled in by purple pencil.

Monsieur [my name, written by hand] *is requested to appear at the Central Police Station of the 3rd Arrondissement, Rue Perrée, on* [in purple:] *November 21 with reference to* [in purple again:] *a matter concerning him. Please bring this form with you.*

I thrust the pink paper into my pocket and went upstairs with the bills and other mail. There had been no rustle of paper, and only a few seconds' delay. Madame Annelet glanced at the envelopes, then looked at me.

"Is that all, Félix?"

I nodded.

"You're sure?"

Isn't it humiliating, at forty-eight, to be found out like a naughty schoolboy? Yet I did not blush, and my face is so flabby that any quivering was concealed in the folds of my skin.

"Why are you hiding the truth from me?"

I held out the summons, and for a moment I suspected my employer of being behind the whole thing, which makes no sense.

"You have no idea why they want you?"

"None."

"You haven't let your dog off the leash or broken any law or regulation? . . . Well, then, we must assume it's the result of Monday's phone call, no?"

That was likely. In any case, it was something connected with the past. The proof of that is that the paper was addressed to the bookshop and not to where I live. I am duly registered at the same local police station, and my address must be in their books. Yet they never bothered to look it up; merely used the address they had been given. But who had given it to them?

"Well, on Thursday you'll know the answer."

This was not the reason, either, why I did not write in this notebook yesterday. I wanted to prove to myself that it had not become a sort of vice. I went for a walk with Bib, who is bewildered whenever I infringe my own rules.

Madame Annelet is not the only one who watches me live. My dog, too, acts as a witness. I lingered later than usual in Place des Vosges, which is not pleasant after night has fallen, because they shut the gates and it's impossible to sit on a bench. Anne-Marie's windows were dark by half past six, which is unusual.

Perhaps I allowed myself a day's respite because I am coming to a difficult period? I have known many men who, apparently at least, retain the same opinion about people and things. Or if they change, it's after a long period of time, and they immediately settle into their new way of thinking.

This is not the case with me, particularly since my trial and imprisonment. I can go further back; it must have started with Anne-Marie. I lived with her for six years. For weeks, for whole months, my opinion of her never varied. Then, all of a sudden, as a result of a minor incident, a remark, an attitude, I would see her for a while with different eyes. Sometimes the change took place twice in a single day.

When I got up and shaved, and left her for the office or for one of my building sites, I would hum to myself happily, under the illusion that I was smiling at her from a distance, and making affectionate contact with her.

By midday, when I went home, I had sometimes become an embittered, disillusioned man, who looked at her as though through a microscope and wondered why she had come into his life.

In my first notebook, I made fun of lovers' meetings.

"I'm trying to understand you."

"To understand what?"

"You must know. . . . You're different from other people. . . ."

Then later on, a few hours or a few days later:

"I wonder how it happened?"

"It had to happen."

"What would have become of us if fate hadn't brought us together?"

"It's a miracle. . . ."

A miracle? It depends on the point of view, and my point of view has changed so often that I have become cautious. I don't know, then, whether my presence on the roof of the Hotel Claridge on the occasion of a military parade was a miracle or a disaster. All I know is that next day I got back to Puteaux at ten in the morning. I was thirty years old. It was not the first time I'd spent a night out. My mother spoke not a word of reproach. Her first question was: "Have you had breakfast?"

I had drunk coffee and eaten croissants in the café next to the hotel. I know that my face was not my usual face.

I was feverish, my skin was taut and my eyes glittering, and I was trying to conceal my excitement.

"Did you have a good time?"

"Very good."

This was not quite the right description, and my mother knew it. I am convinced now that from that moment something changed between us, and my mother foresaw the sequel, whereas I had no inkling of it.

We had drunk a great deal, eaten something or other, and talked a great deal, too, Anne-Marie and I, amid the riotous revels taking place that night around the Champs-Elysées.

I have no idea what happened elsewhere in Paris, for we kept going around in a circle, indifferent to the increasingly disheveled groups that sought to drag us into their dances.

I soon had my arm around her waist to protect her, and we walked close together. Our movements quickly harmonized, and we looked at each other from time to time, so that each could see in the other's eyes the reflection of his or her own enchantment.

Her surname was Varennes. She was born in Lyon, where her father, before the war, had been a journalist. As soon as the Germans invaded Holland, he had foreseen what was to come and had taken his family to London. In 1940, Anne-Marie, who was an only child, was seventeen. She still had to pass her second *bachot*.

They found a two-room apartment in Pimlico, close to an open-air market rather like those in Paris. Her father found work at the BBC; her mother gave French lessons.

All this became entangled in my mind with the parade of troops we had been watching. So did the blitz. She told me a lot about the blitz: the sirens, the noise of airplanes in the sky, the bombs, and the buildings that toppled down after swaying for a moment.

"What were you doing during that time?"

I still used the formal *vous*. *Tu* came only about four or five o'clock in the morning.

"I was learning English. My father had promised to get me into the Free French offices."

He had not had time to. He and his wife were buried, with others, under the ruins of a church they were passing on their way to a shelter.

"I was supposed to go out with them. I don't know why I decided at the last minute to stay behind."

I wanted to know everything. I asked one question after another. We walked till our feet ached. We would go into a bar and drink. Dancing went on all around us and, even when we only stood watching, we followed the rhythms and felt the excitement.

"Monsieur Desmarais, who knew my father well, gave me a job in his office. He was head of a whole department."

"How old is he?"

My question made her laugh.

"I don't know, I never asked him."

"Young or old?"

"Neither old nor young. Thirty-five, maybe."

"Was his wife with him in London?"

"No. He got out through Calais in the very early days, and his wife hadn't been able to join him."

"And you became his secretary?"

"Not immediately. A few months later."

I have never seen him, and in all probability I never will. I don't know what became of him. I have no idea

of his physical appearance—tall or short, dark or fair—
and yet, for years, he was the man who loomed largest
in my thoughts. Even today, I am not sure that I don't
detest him.

He was a wartime colonel and chief of some department or other when we watched the parade from the
Hotel Claridge. Later he became an undersecretary of
state, but I never saw his photograph in the paper, and
with the first change of government he disappeared from
the political scene.

Night was passing. The bars were still as full and as
noisy as ever. From time to time we danced, like everyone
else. We found ourselves back on the sidewalk when the
roofs were beginning to be outlined against a paler sky,
flushed with pink.

I didn't dare ask her the question. She must have
thought of it herself. I was convinced that if we parted
now, it would be all over, that I would be left with merely
the memory of a rather crazy night.

"You're not tired?"

"Not at all."

I almost suggested going to the Bois de Boulogne to
watch the sun rise. We walked back and forth in front
of the Claridge, each time postponing the decision, while
the doorman kept his eyes on us.

"He's getting on my nerves!" she suddenly burst out.
"He seems to be wondering if we're going to make up
our minds."

I urged her forward, gently, toward the revolving door,
and we found ourselves in the deserted lobby.

"Which floor?" asked the elevator boy.

"Sixth," she replied.

I was afraid, physically, agonizingly afraid that something would happen to keep us from going through with it. We went along ever narrower corridors to the back of the hotel. I looked at the shoes outside bedroom doors. She stopped me to point out a pair of tan leather boots beside a woman's shoes with inordinately high heels.

"Who is it?" I asked.

She shrugged her shoulders, implying ignorance.

"A general, for sure!"

She opened her door. I closed it behind us and, without a word, flung myself on her. Did she, too, have a feeling that it was important, that what we were doing now would transform our whole lives?

Without meaning to, I was tense, fierce, almost cruel. I wanted to hurt her, and I hugged her as though to crush the life out of her.

Afterward, we looked at one another as though asking the same question. We were pale with emotion. There was no lightness in our smiles.

"What floor is Desmarais on?"

"The second . . . He moves when high officials or new delegations arrive. . . . You can't be sure, when you go out in the morning, that you'll find your things in the same room."

"Has he been up here?"

She understood.

"No."

"And in London?"

"Yes."

"When you were seventeen?"

"A little later."

"In the office?"

"In his room at the Savoy."

"Was it the first time?"

"I was a virgin, yes."

"And it went on?"

"For a few months."

Why was my throat constricted, my chest shaken by spasms?

"Have there been others?"

"Of course."

"And now?"

She turned her head away. We were lying side by side, and I was holding her hand.

"It seems to upset you, and it's so unimportant!"

"Us, too?"

"I don't know yet. Perhaps not."

And so, like other people, we had come to feel different. Our night together was different. We had done the same as everyone else, but it was for different reasons!

"When was the last time?"

"Last week. Wednesday."

"Desmarais?"

I stubbornly harked back to him.

"No. An English airman."

"Is he still in Paris?"

"He rejoined his squadron next day."

I couldn't have cared less about the English airman and the rest.

"And with Desmarais?"

"That ended a long time ago."

"Why?"

"No special reason. It just came to an end."

"Do you want to see *me* again?"

"I'm a little afraid to."

How sincere was she? And I myself? How much was due to alcohol, to the atmosphere created by the parades and the hordes of celebrating soldiers?

We talked without ever coming to the end of our curiosity and, when we embraced once again, we made love in a grave and slightly saddened way.

"Was it like this with . . ."

Knowing what name I was going to utter, she laid her finger on my lips and shook her head, holding back tears.

Later, I rang for a waiter, who brought us a bottle of whisky and some mineral water. It was broad daylight. The room was narrow, quite devoid of luxury, one of those rooms set aside in grand hotels for guests' chauffeurs.

"Why haven't you married?"

"I've never met a woman I wanted to marry."

"Do you live by yourself?"

"With my mother."

I forget what it was that made us laugh again, the way we had laughed the previous evening. And it was in laughter that our bodies came together finally, while the hotel filled with noises and footsteps.

"You see! I've stopped being jealous. I love you!"

I didn't ask myself if it was true or not.

"I love you too," she answered, with the same look in her eyes.

"Tonight?"

"Perhaps."

"At our little bar on Rue de Ponthieu?"

For we already had *our* little bar, the first we had been into.

"Eight o'clock?"

Wearing pajamas and a blue dressing gown with white dots, she went with me as far as the elevator.

"I suppose you're going to bed?" my mother asked me.

I was not sleepy. I was still wildly excited. Nevertheless, I fell asleep at last, and when I woke, about three in the afternoon, I had a painful hangover.

POOR OLD BIB! Forgive me. After twice hiding your ball half-heartedly, without bothering to look for a difficult place, I pretended not to understand that you still wanted to play. You did not insist, but, instead of going to sleep on the bed, you subsided under the table at my feet. I feel that you are uneasy about all these changes in our habits. Are you wondering, as men do, what the future has in store for you?

You're *my* dog. Are you conscious of belonging to me, or do I, on the contrary, exist, in your opinion, solely in order to feed you, take you for walks, and play with you? The question is not really so absurd. I ask myself much wilder ones.

It has suddenly struck me: the tricks you perform so readily and that amuse me were not taught you by me; you had an earlier master, who took pains to teach them to you, or found pleasure in doing so. It never occurred to me to be jealous of him.

"I want her for my own!"

By the third day, the second, perhaps the first, I wanted her for my own, so desperately that I clenched my fists and scowled at passers-by in the street as if the world was conspiring to take her from me.

For my own! What does it mean, exactly? The exclusive use of her body? I should have protested indignantly if I had been told that. I wanted the whole of her, not only her present being, but her past and future beings.

I have even, on occasion, felt jealous of her father, because he had known her as a little girl, and she had spoken of him with admiration and affection.

"Daddy was like you, strong and calm. I had the feeling that as long as he was there I had nothing to be afraid of."

I made the same impression on everyone: strong and calm.

"I want her for my own!"

And I used to ask her suspiciously, as soon as we met again in our little bar, now restored to its normal routine:

"Have you been seeing him?"

"He dictated letters to me for an hour."

"Nothing else?"

"Of course not!"

Desmarais, as usual. I am not certain today that if he had not existed, I would not have invented some other ghost.

How could I secure her more exclusively for myself? How could I feel certain of possessing her? I used to bruise her, crush her; I made myself suffer, and I was not averse to seeing her at dawn emptied of tears, her voice hoarse with sobbing, her face wan and swollen, with red marks on it.

What did I want from her, in addition to what she gave me? I have been trying to recall my life and to give a fairly faithful picture of it. It remains, nonetheless, basically false, because I am the only one who knows about it. And I am no longer sure what is true and what is less true. If I were to live another ten or twenty years, the past would probably appear to me in quite a different light.

"Tell me about your life in Lyon."

"At what age?"

At every age! But why, for heaven's sake, why this desperate desire to own another human being? And what about her—must I not belong to her, too? Would she not become jealous of my mother, with whom I was still living?

She did, in fact, become so later, but for a different reason.

"Listen, Anne-Marie. If I asked you to leave him . . . ?"

Desmarais, of course, who represented the past, the enemy, the obstacle to be overthrown.

"Do you want me to look for a different job?"

"No."

A job implied men, one man at least, and part of her days spent without me, in an atmosphere about which I knew nothing.

"I want you to be my wife."

"I'm not that already?"

"To be my wife legally; I want us to live together and never be parted."

"Aren't you afraid, Félix?"

"Of what?"

"Of making a mistake. You've known me for eight days."

"I love you. I know that I'm incapable of living without you."

Like everybody else, of course. And presumably this love was as exceptional as everybody else's. Nothing else

125

mattered. My mother sighed as she watched me. Even the workmen exchanged winks behind the back of a boss who was now exultant, now sullen and unsociable.

"When can you leave him?"

"Whenever I like. He doesn't need me any more. He's got all the staff he needs."

"Tomorrow, then?"

"I'll speak to him tomorrow morning."

"I'll find you a room in Neuilly, and then I'll only have to cross the bridge."

"You know, Félix, my parents left me a little money. You won't need to keep me."

She said it with a laugh, but it was enough to set me off again.

"You forget you belong to me."

"That doesn't mean that . . ."

That what? I was asking her for a couple of months, to prepare my mother—as if she hadn't already prepared herself!—to fix up a pleasanter apartment in the old house, and to publish the banns. Was it important to know which of us was going to pay the rent for the room?

"I have something to tell you, Mother."

"You're going to get married."

"You've guessed."

"When?"

"As soon as possible. In six weeks."

"Are you intending to go and live somewhere else?"

"Why? Unless you dislike the idea, we'll live upstairs."

"When are you bringing her to meet me?"

"Whenever you like. I didn't bring her before because she's scared of you. She's shy."

"Really?"

Hadn't my mother followed the course of our relationship from day to day, and didn't she know that at our first meeting I had stayed with Anne-Marie until half past nine the following morning. Didn't I spend almost every night out, even when, for form's sake, I crept back noiselessly at dawn to rumple my bed?

I resented the irony her smile betrayed; it reinforced my knowledge that something was now wrong between us.

The meeting took place quite satisfactorily, without any display of bad feeling; we all remained on guard.

"Since you've lived in England, you must like tea. Milk or lemon?"

And I, meanwhile, was dreading some untoward incident, some blunder on the part of one or the other of them.

"What do you think of her, Mother?"

"She's charming. She isn't quite as I had imagined her."

"What do you mean?"

"I pictured her fair, and taller, I don't know why. She dresses well."

"Very simply."

We had a quiet wedding, without inviting all and sundry, not even my sister, Louise, and her husband. I insisted on having Victor for my witness, and Fernand Dinaire, the foreman, was Anne-Marie's.

She had no relatives in Paris and knew no one there, apart from her former boss and some other people who had returned from London. Before the war, she had been in Paris only once, at the age of fifteen, with her father and mother.

We spent two weeks on the Côte d'Azur, and then, back home, we tried to reorganize our new life. There

were no scenes, no recriminations. On the surface everything went well. We ate our meals with my mother. Anne-
Marie had offered to lend a hand in the office, but it had
soon been made clear to her that this was a forbidden
zone.

We went out a great deal, sometimes more than we
wanted to, because this was the only way to be by ourselves. Not that my mother thrust herself on us at home;
on the contrary, she behaved with exaggerated tact,
which made her presence all the more tangible. Rather
like Bib, who is punishing me by going to sleep out of
sight under the table, instead of in his own place on the
bed, where I'm accustomed to seeing him.

"Do you intend to spend all your life in Puteaux,
Félix?"

"I've never asked myself that question."

"Is it essential for your business?"

"Yes and no. At the point we've now reached, I'd say
no. I have plenty of work going on elsewhere."

I lived in terror of hurting her feelings, distressing or
offending her. She felt the same toward me. She told me
so.

"Are you happy, Félix?"

"I'm the happiest of men. So long as you love me!"

"Do you doubt that?"

"No."

Yes. No. Yes. There were moments when I was not far
from sharing my mother's view. My mother never ex-
pressed an opinion about Anne-Marie, but her attitude,
her glances, above all her silences were more eloquent
than words.

"You'll see, my son, that soon you won't be master in

your own home. She does what she likes with you already, and this is only the beginning. . . ."

Was Anne-Marie really responsible for what followed? We were dining in a restaurant one evening when a blonde young woman rushed up to my wife and embraced her effusively.

"Anne-Marie! It's you!"

"Monique!"

"I often wondered what had become of you."

"Let me introduce my husband."

"Wait till I go get mine."

He had stayed at their table. His name was Cornille, and it was obvious right away that he felt at home everywhere.

"Imagine, Fernand, I've just run into my oldest friend, Anne-Marie Varennes. I've so often told you about her. We used to live next door to each other on the same quay in Lyon, when we were *so* high. . . . But forgive me! . . . I forgot you were married, too. . . . What's your name now?"

"Allard . . . My husband, Félix Allard . . ."

The four of us ate at the same table.

"Tell us! What have you done since I lost sight of you?"

I was going to endure agonies again, as I always did when she talked about London. Cornille, however, let the two women gossip and started asking me questions.

"What's your line?"

"Construction."

"That's good! There's going to be as much building in France as in Baron Haussmann's day, and contractors will make a fortune, just as they did then."

He was far more of a Parisian than I, and I envied his easy manner.

"My line's publicity, but only as a springboard into big business. We're always the first to know what's brewing. . . ."

They lived in a modern apartment on Quai de Passy. We were soon in the habit of going to the theater together, then having supper in a night club, where Cornille would invariably greet prominent personalities and kiss ladies' hands.

The two women telephoned each other every morning and met in the afternoon to do their shopping.

"Are you very fond of Monique?"

"I'm glad to have met her again."

"Because she reminds you of your life in Lyon?"

"No, no, Félix! You're not going to be jealous of Lyon, now? We were only little girls!"

"Weren't you in love with anyone at fourteen or fifteen?"

"My drawing teacher, a white-haired man who smelled of garlic and wore a broad-brimmed hat."

My mother's eyes said:

"It's beginning!"

And Cornille remarked, one evening:

"Say, my friend, why not *tutoyer* each other?"

"If you like."

"Do you mind if I call your wife Anne-Marie?"

A quarter of an hour later he was dancing with her, and I was dancing with Monique.

"You're jealous, aren't you?"

"Is it obvious?"

"Don't worry as far as my husband is concerned. He

always seems to be flirting with every woman. It's his way; he needs to show off."

He was a more fluent and sparkling talker than I was. I longed to be like him, to juggle as he did with life and with people.

"By the way, Félix, we must have a talk one of these days. I have a little idea that could take us a long way, you and me. You've never been to my office. Next time you're on the Champs-Elysées, come up and say hello."

He had to ask me repeatedly, and one morning he called up to say that he simply must see me at three o'clock. When I went there, I saw, in one of the huge pale leather armchairs, a little man in black, unkempt, fat, and greasy-looking, whose sparse black hair lay in streaks across his skull, looking as though it had been painted on.

"My good friend Allard . . . My friend Mimieux . . . You don't know Mimieux, but you're going to know him. . . . One of the best-informed men about what goes on in Paris, whether it's in publishing or in banking, in the ministries or the municipal council . . . He's a sort of *éminence grise*, a go-between. Do you understand?"

No. I did not understand, yet.

Mimieux had globular yellowish eyes and exuded the sickly smell of a diseased liver.

"You're well aware that in order to relieve congestion in Paris . . ."

I still thought this was all idle talk.

"You must know the district of Montesson, near Carrières-sur-Seine?"

"I've been that way."

A quarter of an hour later, maps were spread out on

the desk, and I can still remember the noise from the Champs-Elysées while Cornille was speaking, because it was early summer, and the windows were wide open.

"See this piece of land? We have an option on it, and before six months are up we'll start building luxury apartments there, with a swimming pool. It's to be called the Résidence de la Tour. Fifty-four apartments have already been sold, before the first stone has been laid. The architect, one of the best in Paris, is at work. Mimieux has undertaken to obtain the necessary permits from the ministry and from the municipalities concerned, since we're on the border between two communes.

"What we're asking you today is whether you'll come in with us. You realize that it's a big undertaking, and that there's big money in it. You'll have to find equipment and labor, unless you bring it in from abroad. After these blocks, there'll be others. . . ."

"You've taken me by surprise. . . ."

"I wanted to give you first chance. When can I have your answer?"

"In a week?"

"Say, Monday. That gives you four days. On Sunday we'll go and visit the place with our wives. Of course you'll need new offices, in town preferably. Mimieux will fix you up."

I realized, when I got home, that Anne-Marie had been informed before I had.

"Did Fernand tell you about La Tour?"

"Yes."

"What have you decided?"

"Nothing yet."

"Monique assures me that it's a serious proposition.

And there's a big private bank involved. What's on your mind?"

"Nothing."

"You're feeling reluctant?"

"I don't know."

"Would you mind leaving Puteaux?"

So that, too, had been discussed. I would have not only new offices, but a new apartment as well. Without my mother, obviously!

"By the way, did you know that Monique is pregnant?"

"Her husband didn't mention it."

"She told me yesterday. Wouldn't you like us to have a baby, too?"

You have to choose between one interpretation and another. My mother would doubtless have muttered, "The minx!"

Such a thought sometimes happened to me, but I always promptly blamed myself for it.

A wife of my own! A child of my own!

"Félix!"

"Yes?"

"I love you."

"I love you, too."

"Shall we start now?"

She was laughing, but we were emotionally excited as we flung ourselves on the bed.

"Hush! . . . Quiet! . . . Your mother's just underneath us. . . ."

By two o'clock in the morning, we had almost emptied a bottle of Scotch and were discussing which district we would live in.

Tomorrow, Thursday, at 4:00 P.M., I will know what they want with me at the police station.

Thursday, November 21

WHAT SURPRISED THEM MOST was to see me appear with a dog. Not only the uniformed policemen on the other side of the gray counter, but the people waiting on the seats with their backs against the wall, a dozen or so men and women.

They all began by looking down at Bib's pudgy little form, at my feet and legs. Their gaze traveled upward, taking in my stomach and finally resting insistently on my face. Then it dropped again, to settle on the dog.

What was it that astonished and shocked them so?

I held out my pink paper to one of the policemen, and it was passed from hand to hand, each time provoking a frown and a glance in my direction, until finally somebody took it into another room.

"Sit down."

If only Bib doesn't take it into his head to play dead or turn somersaults! There was no sort of contact between the waiting people and myself. They were silent, true, but, sitting there side by side, they formed a group, with certain things in common. Not with me. I was an outsider.

"You're not like other people. . . ."

I used to be, though, at the time when I enjoyed being told I was not.

Now, I am not; and they all felt it, while we were waiting on the same side of the barrier, tormented by the same uneasiness, the same vague dread that one feels in places such as this.

The ordeal lasted only five minutes. Although my neighbors had arrived before me, my name was the one spoken by a man in plain clothes as he held open a baize-covered door.

I got up, followed by Bib on his leash, and they all continued looking at us with the same curiosity, the man in plain clothes, too, and finally the superintendent, sitting behind his desk.

I am sure he was about to make some remark about the dog, but he changed his mind and indicated a chair.

"Félix Allard? The same who was once convicted of manslaughter and sentenced to five years' hard labor?"

It was starting all over again, just as it had at the time of my trial. I was up against people whose business it is to deal with criminals. That's the word, and I am inevitably bound to use it myself.

They had tried to talk to me in an informal way, as though to one of themselves, particularly the examining magistrate, who could not help showing a certain sympathy for me. Sympathy mingled with curiosity, not with repugnance. I was not made conscious of any repugnance at that time; dislike, rather, and embarrassment.

A man who has killed is no longer one's fellow man. It is almost as if he has ceased to be quite human.

How could he have done it? What does he feel? What is he thinking?

I have perhaps become supersensitive, and I may be deceiving myself. Why do passers-by who know nothing about me or my story, or insignificant people waiting on a police-station bench, look at me as if my presence upset them?

Others my age are also visibly sick men, and I am not the only person who takes a small dog around with him. There are no strange marks on my face.

"I understand you work as assistant at Madame Annelet's bookshop, Boulevard Beaumarchais?"

"I have for the past eight years. I started a few weeks after my release from Melun."

It disturbs me to be looked at like that.

"Do you live by yourself?"

"With my dog."

"Do you have a permanent residence?"

"Close to the bookshop, on Rue des Arquebusiers. I came to register myself at this very station as soon as I moved into my apartment."

He lifted the receiver of an internal telephone, without taking his eyes off me.

"Please check whether a certain Félix Allard . . . Allard, yes, no H . . . is registered as living on Rue des Arquebusiers. . . . Thank you. I have a few questions to ask you, Monsieur Allard. You were a married man and had two children, I believe?"

"I still am. There has been no divorce."

"On your release, you did not go back to your wife. Was this your decision?"

"No."

"Have you seen your wife again?"

"Only from a distance."

"Have you tried to see her?"

"Not exactly. I caught sight of her one day in Place des Vosges, and I learned that she lived there with my son and daughter."

"When did you make this discovery?"

"Shortly after I came to live on Rue des Arquebusiers."

"So you didn't choose this neighborhood in order to be near Place des Vosges?"

"No."

"Didn't you want to see your children again?"

"Perhaps . . . From a distance . . ."

Each of my answers surprised him, and led him a little farther away from the simple truth.

"Have you never tried to speak to them?"

"Never."

"Nor to your wife?"

"No."

"Afraid of getting a bad reception?"

"No."

There was a knock on the door, and the man who had showed me in laid a slip of paper on the desk and went out again. This must be the confirmation of my entry in the local police register.

"I see. . . . I see. . . . So it wasn't deliberate, either, that you came to live close to somebody else? . . . You can guess who I mean?"

I didn't flinch, but I suddenly felt unwell.

"Chance, I am now obliged to believe, brought this other person to live in your neighborhood. . . . This person also has two children, a boy and a girl. . . . Will you tell me, Monsieur Allard, why you follow them in the street, and why you sometimes keep watch in front of the building they live in? . . .

"On Monday, when Madame Cornille learned where you work, she decided to come and see me. . . . She's a calm, level-headed person. You know that, don't you? . . . When her daughter first told her about a stranger she kept meeting, who seemed to know her, she put it down to a schoolgirl's imagination. . . .

"But you followed the brother, too, as far as the Lycée Turgot, and you frequently waited in a little café to see him come out. . . . Do you deny it?"

"No."

"Tell me, then, the reason for this kind of spying."

"It's not a question of spying. I watch them living."

"Why?"

"I want to know what becomes of them. . . ."

"Them in particular?"

"Yes."

"The children of the man you killed?"

For decency's sake, I lowered my head. This, I have learned, is what people expect of me.

"And also, I suppose, what becomes of the woman you have widowed?"

"I beg your pardon."

"For what?"

"I hoped she would not notice me in the crowd. I have changed a lot in thirteen years."

"Madame Cornille caught sight of you below the windows of the lawyer's office where she works, on Rue du Bac."

"I never tried to . . ."

I could not find the words. I was overwhelmed. If Anne-Marie had come to complain of my behavior, I would not have been so affected.

"I'm listening, Monsieur Allard."

"I have nothing to say. . . . I apologize once more. . . . From now on, I'll take care to keep out of their way. . . ."

I hardly recognized my own voice; it came from very deep down.

"I strongly advise you to. You realize, I suppose, that

it is most disagreeable for a woman and her children to endure the presence of the man who . . ."

"Please . . ."

I felt my eyelids swelling. I did not want to cry. He was unaware that he had taken away the little that was left me. He must have assumed that I was troubled by remorse.

"I know that it's not easy, in your position, to get another job and move to another district. So I insist all the more strongly that you must stop annoying this family, to whom you've already done enough harm. . . . Is that quite clear?"

"I promise."

"I hope you'll keep your word. Otherwise, I will be obliged to take severe measures."

He rose, less sure of himself than he would have liked. I got up, too, mumbling:

"Thank you . . ."

For the first time, if Bib had not followed me, dragging his leash behind him, I would have forgotten him.

I went through the room where the people were waiting, and their eyes followed me to the door. The superintendent, it suddenly occurs to me, did not say goodbye. He, too, watched me go, without a word.

I had promised Madame Annelet to return to the shop. My place was being taken by Renée, who, every time a customer came in, had to go up to the mezzanine to find out the price of a book.

I stopped to drink a glass of whisky on the way, and, when my glance fell on Bib, I seemed to be seeing him for the first time.

I took off my coat in the back room. The dog went to take refuge in his place under the counter. Then I went upstairs slowly, and she did not cross-examine me right away. I no longer felt on familiar ground. My last links had just been severed.

"Was it your wife?"

I shook my head.

"The other woman?"

I turned to look at her in stupefaction. I had never told her about Monique's presence in the neighborhood, nor about Daniel and Martine.

"How do you know?"

"I am capable of using the telephone directory, like anyone else. . . . When you began to change . . ."

What has changed about me?

"I asked myself some questions. Then Renée saw you hanging around in front of a certain apartment building. What did she complain of?"

"I don't know."

"You've never tried to speak to her or to the children?"

"Never."

I was so sure, though, that Daniel would come up to me one day! I could have sworn he recognized me, that he was as curious about me as I was about him.

"Does she still feel bitter against you?"

"They didn't tell me so."

"Why did she go to the police?"

"So that I'd stop following them."

I have undergone too many interrogations not to confess right away to something true that will inevitably be extracted from me in the end.

I have stopped struggling now. I give way, perhaps out of laziness. This conversation frightened me, because I guessed what Madame Annelet was aiming at.

She did not beat around the bush.

"Are you in love with her, Félix?"

Why spoil everything deliberately? I bore no grudge against the superintendent, who had merely done his duty. But she, with her bony shoulders, her heavily painted fortuneteller's face, and her glittering black eyes . . . Wasn't she seized with a moment's panic? I was staring at her, with my teeth clenched, and I am almost sure I felt tempted to clutch her throat in my big hands.

"Were you already, before . . . ?" she insisted.

I was being left with nothing, not even the right to daydream. I did not answer. I went downstairs, and almost went on out the door, without my coat, just the way, a short while before, I had nearly forgotten Bib at the police station. However, I waited behind the counter until the clock showed twenty-five past six, and then meekly went up the spiral stairs to take her the envelope of money.

"Listen, Félix . . ."

"I'm listening."

"Look at me. Are you paying attention?"

"Yes."

"Promise me to be here tomorrow morning."

What was she afraid of? She needn't worry. I had no such intention.

"Why?"

"Because I need you."

How different words can sound, over a few years' distance! I used to say to Anne-Marie:

"You'll never leave me?"

"Why do you ask such a foolish question?"

"Because I need you!"

"I need you, too, Félix!"

It was not true for either of us, but we did not know that.

I have eaten nothing this evening. I had only to grill the meat and warm up the cooked vegetables I had bought this morning. But I hadn't the heart to do it, and neither did I want to go and sit in a restaurant, where I'd be sure everyone was watching me. Besides, I am not hungry. I prepared Bib's food. He is increasingly puzzled by my behavior.

I may as well admit it at once, since it will probably be evident to anyone who may read these pages someday: I bought, on my way home, a bottle of Burgundy marc. You can't buy whisky in the small local groceries that stay open in the evening.

I have drunk one glass. I have poured myself another, which is standing in front of me. Once, and once only, in my student days, I got drunk on marc with some friends, and I have never felt so wretched as I did the next morning. Except, possibly, the day after meeting Anne-Marie on the roof of the Claridge.

What is there to stop me from drinking? Not concern for my health. And wasn't the love between Anne-Marie and me born of alcohol? Didn't we keep that up, both of us? Didn't those jealous fits of mine, which drove me to wound and sully her, break out when I was drunk?

I feel tempted to burn my two notebooks and begin all over again, but this time really get to the bottom of things, probing truth to the bone. Not only the truth about myself, but the truth about others, too.

Nobody would understand. It would involve becoming *me*, getting into my skin, and who would want to do that? I don't feel at ease myself in this sallow, flabby skin which no longer fits me. Does Madame Annelet realize what she has just done to me?

I have emptied the second glass, and since, for the past thirteen years, I have drunk almost nothing but water, I already feel the effect of it. My head is reeling a little, and I see the words I am writing as though through dirty spectacles.

I have not yet spoken about the Félix Allard of the years between 1946 and 1951. He's a man I can scarcely recognize, and I am ashamed of recalling him. Is that his fault? If not, whose is it?

Can you imagine the first thing that idiot did? It was to ask Cornille for the address of his tailor, to order some suits for himself! Because in the set into which he was about to move, people dressed differently. Always that concern with being different! Whether at Fouquet's or Maxim's or other fashionable restaurants or night clubs, the cut of one's clothes served as a password.

And the make of one's car, too. And the way one walked in and went to one's table, smiling to acquaintances, with a slight wave of the hand. And the way one studied the menu and spoke to the headwaiter . . .

I had not played at being a clever schoolboy or a good student; I had *been* both. I have said so before, but it doesn't matter. Nor had I played at being the tough, blunt businessman of Puteaux, or the lover and husband obsessed with jealousy.

Presumably the rest, too, was something I had in me. I took myself seriously. I handled a lot of business. I lived in a modern building in Neuilly, just across the river from Puteaux, in an apartment like those of the film producers, stars, and industrialists who were my neighbors.

I used to meet them again at the theater and at late suppers, then at Megève over Christmas and New Year's, at Cannes or Antibes for Easter, at Deauville later, and, when the shooting season opened, in the Sologne.

I had taken up shooting! Anne-Marie and I went to buy ourselves guns at Gastinne-Renette's, and we were given lessons in the basement. I also learned to play bridge and poker. I even took riding lessons in the Bois de Boulogne.

I had my offices on Rue Marbeuf, with the same kind of chairs Cornille had. When Philippe was born, his nurse wore an English nanny's uniform.

This kind of life went on for five years. Time passed quickly. But I must really play with Bib for a moment. I haven't the right to disappoint him, and I may still need him.

"ASK MIMIEUX . . ."

"Mimieux will fix that. . . ."

"Mimieux's looking after things. . . ."

He reminded one of a toad. His handshake was moist and soft. He lived somewhere at the top of Boulevard Voltaire, but I don't believe he ever entertained anyone there.

There was a Madame Mimieux, whom nobody ever saw either, and I suppose she must have been as ugly as he was. They had no children.

Mimieux did not own a car and traveled only by Métro, which enabled him to keep his appointments punctually. He would draw his watch from his waistcoat pocket, its lid would spring open, then he would shut it again with a snap. I always saw him wearing the same black suit, and if he ever had a new pair of shoes, one wouldn't have guessed it.

"The first thing to do is to form a joint-stock company. . . ."

"But . . ."

"Don't raise objections until I've explained it to you. . . ."

He had begun at the age of sixteen in some obscure legal office on Rue Coquillière, near Les Halles. He had read only one book in his life, *The Civil Code*, which he knew by heart, and he was said to be the best-informed man in Paris on corporation law and the way to make use of it.

He convinced me, and I went to talk to my mother.

"Listen to this, Mother . . ."

"When are you moving?"

"That's not what I want to talk to you about. You must understand that I'm anxious to enlarge the business. Wasn't that what Father did when Grandfather retired? We're entering a period . . ."

"Where do you intend to move to?"

"It's essential that the office be in Paris. I'll keep the old warehouses, and perhaps build others. As for you, if you'd like me to leave a foreman and a few workers . . ."

"It's kind of you to have thought of it, but I'm feeling tired, and the rest will be good for me."

"As regards our arrangements . . ."

"As long as you leave me the house and give me enough to live on for the rest of my days . . ."

"I've inquired in the right quarters: to secure the funds I need, particularly credit from the bank, it's essential to

146

form a joint-stock company. Of course, you'll be allotted shares. . . ."

"No, Félix. Thank you very much, but I'd rather not be mixed up in all that."

This was the first warning note. I did not heed it. The second was sounded by Monsieur Beauchef, my accountant.

"Don't take it amiss, Monsieur Félix, but I wouldn't feel at ease in your new concern."

"What do you intend to do?"

"I'll go back to my former clients—small tradesmen and craftsmen who need my help once a week."

Monique's pregnancy was nearing its end, and Anne-Marie was not pregnant yet. We still went out as a foursome. Cornille would dance with my wife while Monique and I sat watching, which I did not mind, because I have never been fond of dancing.

"Anne-Marie has astonishing vitality!"

I refrained from saying:

"Just like Fernand!"

The same kind of animation inspired them both. Contact with somebody from outside acted on each of them like a spark. To go into a restaurant, to meet some acquaintance on the street was enough to set them going. In the space of one second, they became dazzling and indefatigable.

"Did Mimieux tell you about the shares?"

"He spoke to me about them yesterday."

"What do you think?"

"You know I know nothing about it."

When Mimieux explained the details of a deal, it all seemed clear and legitimate. I could find no objection to raise. It was only later, before I fell asleep, that doubts and scruples occurred to me.

"Don't forget he has started more than forty companies, and never had the slightest trouble."

Since I was the contractor, my name did not appear on the prospectus of the La Tour Building Society, as we had called it. A retired general was chairman of the board of directors. Nevertheless, I held one-third of the shares.

It is true, however, that issuing new shares for my own business had been blocked by the bank. I had been obliged to visit Rouen to see my sister, who had not yet received the full amount of her inheritance.

I found nothing unusual about these transactions, any more than about living on Boulevard Richard-Wallace, opposite Bagatelle Park.

Mimieux, always Mimieux, had produced a couple of bulldozers for me, as well as a crane and an excavator, which the American army had brought over for building wartime airfields.

"We've done it this time, Félix! You can open a bottle of champagne!"

"Done what?"

"Can't you guess?"

I looked more closely at Anne-Marie.

"Really? You're pregnant?"

I loved her. I couldn't have helped loving her. We got wildly excited, and called the Cornilles, then went to spend the rest of the evening with them.

Every day I drove in my big American car to La Tour, where construction was going on. Sketches had been exhibited in a shop window on the Champs-Elysées, rented at Cornille's suggestion, and four months later every apartment was sold, while I was still casting the floors of the third story and digging the swimming pool.

I gave Anne-Marie a small car. Philippe was born. Then I presented my wife with a diamond and my son with the most expensive English perambulator. From our windows, we were able, before long, to watch him with his nurse on the other side of the railings around the Bois de Boulogne. Leaning out, I could also see my huge car, with Anne-Marie's tiny elegant one behind it.

"Are you happy?"

"Aren't you?"

Of course I said yes. I had no time not to be happy. All day, appointments and visits to building sites succeeded one another without pause. Six people were now working in my office. I frequently lunched in town with architects or suppliers, or with Cornille.

"Is that you, Anne-Marie? Sorry, dear, but I can't get home for lunch."

"Poor lamb, you're working too hard! Is it still all right for this evening?"

Of course! Every evening there was something planned: a dinner, the opening of a new night club, a gala performance.

I must have loved her, since I was jealous!

During her pregnancy she sometimes asked me:

"How are you managing, poor Félix?"

Because the doctor had advised against sexual relations after the third month.

"I never think about it."

"You're sure? You don't sometimes want to go and see some other woman?"

I did; I went. Among others, I went to bed with the

149

secretary of one of the architects, because she had big breasts, and I was surprised to hear her burst out laughing at the climax. Near the Madeleine, I knew some quiet bars where one could be sure of finding pretty girls.

"Do you think you can last till the end?"

"I'm sure of it."

Why did I feel compelled to lie?

"She belongs to me!"

A recurrent theme. And I, theoretically, belonged to her, and Philippe belonged to us. So, later on, did Nicole, born a few months after the Cornilles' second child. It was like a race between the two families. We made a joke of it.

"Next time *we're* going to set the example!"

The first mink coat was a Christmas present. Monique had had hers a year earlier. I had become a customer of shops on Faubourg Saint-Honoré, Place Vendôme, and elsewhere, in which at one time I would never have ventured to set foot. I ordered shirts and pajamas by the dozen. I signed checks. If I was in any difficulty, Cornille would say:

"Go and see Mimieux."

And something was arranged. Everything was fixed. To advertise the second group of buildings, in a park near Versailles, we bought a whole page in the leading newspapers. We needed ready money to finish La Tour, where we had considerably overspent our estimates. That was Mimieux's business.

In the evenings and on weekends and holidays, we lived in another world. The upper ten thousand? Perhaps less, perhaps more. Successful industrialists, doctors, lawyers, businessmen.

We were successful. Cornille rented a place in the

forest of Orléans, at Ingrannes, and had a modern lodge built there, with huge kennels and stables. We went there for weekends, arriving on Saturday afternoons at first, and then on Friday evenings.

All this seems cloudy and unreal, perhaps because I've just drunk a fourth glass of marc. I'm going in a circle. Since I began these notebooks, I've been wasting my time, really, through not daring to attack the real problem.

Until I was thirty, the word *love* had no meaning for me. Then it came to mean that fever that possessed me when I met Anne-Marie, and the torture I inflicted on myself through jealousy. That I inflicted on her, too—by what right, I now wonder.

Was her past any concern of mine? Was I entitled to call her to account? Had I been in London during the blitz, when she suddenly found herself alone there? What had I been doing then? What was I still doing, and not only when pregnancy made her unavailable?

That did not prevent me, during my jealous attacks, from treating her like a despicable creature and deliberately trying to strip her of any self-respect.

"Forgive me, Félix. It hurts me so to know that you're suffering because of me. . . ."

And while she was dancing with Cornille, or when, late at night, they started one of their interminable conversations, Monique and I exchanged glances. We must have looked like accomplices; we were rather like mothers affectionately watching their children at play.

"They're indefatigable, the two of them!"

Evenings never seemed long enough. I would feel sleepy, because I had to get up early, and so did Monique. We suffered patiently, united in a kind of freemasonry.

I loved Anne-Marie, and Monique loved her Fernand.
She would say, quite calmly, with a touch of resignation:

"It's not his fault. He needs to feel life all around him.
He's bubbling over with energy!"

She was the daughter of a history professor, who, now
retired and still living in Lyon, was writing a fat book
about the Merovingians. Wasn't that the career I had
chosen? It seemed to me another link between her and
me.

"I'll wonder all my life why he married me, when I'm
such a bourgeoise."

I almost expected to hear her add:

"He ought to have married someone like Anne-
Marie!"

I often thought of that, not as a possible reality, but as
a purely theoretical conception. And it did not shock me,
although I worked myself into a frenzy at the mere name
of Desmarais.

Nobody suspected or mentioned this, fortunately. Nobody guessed it, except for that frightful witch Madame
Annelet.

Not even Monique, I am now almost convinced. We
were good friends who understood one another's slightest
word or glance.

"When I think that Fernand could have the prettiest
girls in Paris!"

He missed no opportunity of doing so, but it was not
my business to betray him. He used to tell me about his
adventures, and often needed me for an alibi.

"Do you mind if I call Monique and tell her I'm lunch-
ing with you?" As he did so, he would give me a wink.

"Did you notice that little brunette yesterday at the

Nouvelle Eve? I managed to get hold of her phone number, and we're having lunch together. Above all, don't mention it to Anne-Marie; you can never be sure with women."

I did not mention it to Anne-Marie. She and I rented a villa at Deauville.

This state of things lasted for five years, and I wonder what I would be like today if it had gone on longer. My mother fell ill. I used to go and see her from time to time in the old house, where Aunt Julie, with whom she was now reconciled, often kept her company. For reasons of tact, my wife went with me only on New Year's visits.

"Are you still happy, Félix?"

"Of course, Mother. You're the one who should be inquired after. How's that kidney trouble?"

"Still a bother. Do you know who's been looking after me since our old Chollet died? His son, who was a doctor at one of the hospitals. He's taken over the practice."

I saw him, a tall, solemn, rather gauche young fellow.

"Is it serious, doctor?"

"Unfortunately, yes. I've had your mother examined by one of my former professors. He advises against an operation. It would mean useless torture for her, and she'd only gain a month or two."

She dragged on for a year, with Frida by her side, and Aunt Julie, who, because of the wall in the courtyard, had to come by way of Rue Voltaire. At the funeral, I was surprised to see Monsieur Beauchef, whose new address I didn't know, and so I hadn't notified him of her death.

I'm still going in a circle. I've nearly emptied that bottle. I thought alcohol would excite me, give me some extra energy, or at least take away my reluctance and my inhibitions.

I have never felt so weak and listless. If it weren't for Madame Annelet's remarks running through my head, I would immediately swallow the two tubes of sleeping pills I have put aside, and the whole thing would be over.

She managed to frighten me, the bitch! The thought that I might change my mind when it was too late . . . Here, above all, in a house where Bib and I are alone at night . . . It's raining. I hear the drops falling on the skylight over my head.

The superintendent was not too harsh with me. He must have felt sorry for me. It was Monique who had gone to ask him to intervene. Anne-Marie had made no complaint. It's hard to imagine that she never caught sight of me in Place des Vosges.

Why should she bother about me? She has remade her life in her own way. A woman like Anne-Marie is never in trouble for very long. She has her family on Place des Vosges. In her boutique on Faubourg Saint-Honoré, she has a partner, a man some four or five years younger.

I have seen them. I know about it. She is still young, but she'll soon reach the danger point, and then her drama will begin, as Madame Annelet's once did. She'll fight even more fiercely than the old bookseller.

This is the woman I wanted to belong to me, to me alone. Her children are mine. I have sometimes doubted that, and sought to hold someone else responsible for them, as an excuse for looking at them with such curiosity.

Philippe is like me at his age, and that causes me

embarrassment rather than pleasure. It's impossible to say as yet whom Nicole will be like. For the time being, she reminds me of my sister, Louise.

As for Daniel, he is the image of his mother, with her smile and her calm manner. It was partly because of this that I kept hoping to see him come into the bookshop and ask me for some book or other, so he could have an opportunity of studying me at close quarters. Long before the superintendent spoke to me, I was almost sure he had recognized me. And yet he was only five when it happened.

I had bounced him on my knee, as Cornille had bounced my children on his.

I reek of marc. I feel I'm sweating it through every pore. My mouth is thick, my hand heavy, my head full of muddled thoughts. I am drunk. A sick, drunken old man writing under a skylight through which from time to time there falls a large, cold drop of water. I don't give a damn for my dog, I don't give a damn for anybody, Madame Annelet, Anne-Marie, the children, or Monique. Exactly! I don't give a damn for Monique!

I imagine her at the police station, perfectly calm, sure of her rights. Of course! She works in a lawyer's office! Does she sleep with him, too, as Anne-Marie does with Antonio? My wife's partner is named Antonio!

"Please excuse my bothering you, Superintendent. There's a man in the neighborhood . . ."

The bitch! Surely she realizes. Has she understood nothing? Did I really bother her so much? Did she think that my presence in the street was enough to pollute the air and contaminate Daniel and Martine?

"At night he walks up and down the sidewalk on the

other side of the street with his dog, staring up at our windows, and when it rains he takes shelter in a doorway. . . ."

It was all I had left.

Damn! *Merde!* I must go and be sick, and that idiot Bib will gaze at me reproachfully again.

Monday, November 25

I HAVE JUST SPENT two and a half days in bed, three days without writing. At one point I decided not to add another word to these notebooks, and to destroy them. I had not been quite sincere when I pretended not to know for whom they were intended. In my heart, I was thinking of Monique. Absurd as it may seem, it was a kind of declaration of love, of a love that really *was* unlike other kinds. I would have been quite glad if Daniel, too, had read these pages someday.

Now I have recovered my calm, my peace of mind, or, more exactly, my indifference. I believe I am once more capable of looking at myself, not from within, which might incline me to indulgence, but from without, as others see me.

I will try to remain cold and lucid to the end.

It was on Thursday that the superintendent unwittingly dealt me the hardest blow I have yet had to endure, and Madame Annelet, as I might have expected, took advantage of it to finish me off.

I drank. I have no desire to reread what I wrote on Thursday night. I went to bed, and at six o'clock Bib woke me. Still dazed, which seldom happens to me, I got up to open the door for him, and it was then that everything began to spin around me, and I collapsed on the floor like some large insect.

It was not directly due to the marc. I have had other spells of dizziness during the last few months, less violent, which forced me to stop still in the street but allowed me to stay on my feet. It's agonizing the first few times, but you get used to it. It has nothing to do with my illness. It's just an extra infirmity.

I did not lose consciousness, and what I chiefly felt was humiliation, even though nobody was there except my dog, who looked at me without understanding and uttered little yelps.

At first he must have thought it was a new game. I got painfully to all fours. I tried to stand up. Then, giving up the attempt, I managed, with cautious movements, to reach my bed.

It was raining. It's still raining. For four days a fine invisible rain has been falling, and I have mechanically watched the water trickling down the panes. Lying in bed, I played at guessing if one of the streams would run to the left or to the right, and I was almost invariably wrong.

Bib ran around in a circle, impatiently, and whimpered. I could do nothing for him. He could do nothing for me. We both had to wait. We heard the girls invading the workshop on the second floor and the trucks unloading supplies on the ground floor.

Madame Annelet must have thought, when I failed to appear at eight o'clock, that I had at last committed suicide. I am no longer afraid of the word, nor ashamed of it either. At half past eight, as I had foreseen, she sent Renée to me, and Bib was able to dash out into the street.

"So you're ill now! Have you sent for the doctor, at least?"

What for? And how could I, since I have no telephone?

"I must go and tell Madame. Is there anything I can do for you?"

I had a hangover, but as long as I lay quietly it was not painful or even unpleasant. She made me some coffee, which, I thought, tasted horrible. She left. At about ten, she came back with a pot of vegetable broth.

"Madame has called your doctor. He'll come to see you as soon as he can."

Bib did not get back on the bed. He settled down in the farthest corner of the room, as though he were sulking.

"Shall I light the fire?"

"If you want to."

Renée went back and forth between Boulevard Beaumarchais and Rue des Arquebusiers all day. She is twenty-two; she'll live long after me. She must think I've already had my share. Perhaps she wonders why I'm not yet dead, and resents my inflicting extra work on her.

I would not, of my own accord, have sent for Dr. Heim, who lives on Boulevard Richard-Lenoir. But since Madame Annelet had notified him, I expected to see him arrive at any moment.

It was not until three in the afternoon that I heard his car stop outside. Then a door was slammed, and his footsteps sounded on the stairs.

"I couldn't come any earlier. I've had a very busy day."

I might have died meanwhile. But of course there are others in the same state, younger men, women, or children who, as the saying is, have their lives before them.

I understood him. I understood his attitude toward me, which is strictly professional, with no attempt to establish any human contact. He examined me, looked at his watch as he held my wrist, took my blood pressure, felt my abdomen, and merely frowned.

"What happened?"

"I got up as usual, and immediately felt dizzy and fell."

"Have you been following my instructions?"

"No."

As a man, I don't interest him; as a patient, hardly at all, because he knows there is nothing to be done.

Why should he feel sympathy for me? Who could be fond of me, even in the slightest degree? The sight of me tends, instead, to make people uneasy, as if they guessed that within the mass of quivering flesh that I have become decay has already set in and is slowly doing its work.

Faced with such a spectacle, they sometimes seem to be asking themselves:

"Is he going to shout or groan, bite things or burst into tears?"

I don't shout or bite, nor do I burst into tears. I shed no tears in the police station.

Dr. Heim noticed the half-empty bottle of marc.

"Was it you who . . . ?"

Who else could have been drinking in my attic?

"Last night?"

I don't care if he feels disgust or contempt for me. I am back to where I was so short a while ago—two weeks, if I'm not mistaken—before I met my two foolishly radiant monsters climbing the steps to Sacré-Coeur.

I had vowed not to yield to sentimentality. I'm afraid I may have given way to it once or twice. The time I have just spent in bed has put things back in their right places. Since I have begun to tell my story, I will finish it, without self-pity.

On Saturday, I tried three times to get up, carefully, holding on to the bed, and I realized it was useless.

Renée came back several times, after hanging on the bookshop door the notice that says: "Closed until . . . o'clock." As with certain calendars and parking meters, you turn a cardboard or metal disk and a figure appears in the slit.

On Sunday, I was able to move around in my room and I told Renée not to bother coming in the afternoon, but to take her day off as usual. Madame Annelet and I each stayed in our holes, while thousands of people queued up outside the movie theaters.

Where had I got to? It doesn't matter. I'm not attempting to stick the pieces together again. The situation was bound to break up. We were living in the midst of so much money we didn't know what to do with it, yet we were always short of it.

"Ask Mimieux . . ."

It couldn't last indefinitely, and I sometimes longed for the end to come as soon as possible.

"Don't you think, Fernand, that . . ."

"Oh, you've always been a pessimist. Since Mimieux . . ."

Mimieux waved no danger signal. He merely asked for my signature from time to time, and I had gotten in the habit of signing anything. It was all too complicated for me.

"What is it? What are they doing in your office?"

I had seen unfamilar faces, severe and unfriendly, in the accounting department of the Building Society, where I had gone to see Cornille.

"Experts from the Financial Section of the Public Prosecutor's Office."

"Does that mean it's dangerous?"

"Mimieux swears it's only a routine inspection, and they'll find nothing out of line."

Unvaryingly impassive and polite, they studied our books for a whole week. Then they turned up at my office on Rue Marbeuf.

"Aren't our finances in order?"

"In business, one's never in order. So long as Mimieux says there's nothing to be alarmed about . . ."

We got an increasing number of telephone calls from clients who had bought apartments and were worried by seeing that work had not yet begun. A paragraph in a weekly paper started a slight panic. Mimieux, still traveling by Métro, grew more cautious about handing out money to Cornille and me, as well as to our chief accountants.

As for Anne-Marie, she went on living as if nothing had happened. We went out more than ever.

"It would be bad not to show ourselves. People would assume that . . ."

Monique occasionally gave me a questioning look. I was not yet in love with her, or, if I was, I was not conscious of it. It was only at Melun that I had time to reflect and to clarify my thoughts and feelings.

April came. For once, we had not gone to spend the Easter holidays on the Côte d'Azur, because the Public Prosecutor's Office had politely requested us not to leave Paris and to keep ourselves available.

Spring was early that year, sunny and warmer than in previous years, and I can still see myself bringing home the first strawberries, set out on cotton wool like jewels in a case. I could not find Anne-Marie. I went into our room to change. Having no more cigarettes in my pocket,

I opened her bag, which she had left on a small table, to take one from the gold case I had given her.

I almost paid no attention to the key my fingers touched at the bottom of the bag. Its shape surprised me. It was neither a car key nor the key to our apartment. I was shocked. It hurt, although I was not really surprised. I immediately thought of Cornille, and I knew. I put the key back and, after a moment's pause to compose my face, I went into the nursery, where Anne-Marie was playing with the children.

"Strawberries! The first!"

On two afternoons, at the time she usually went out, supposedly to meet Monique or to do the shopping, I waited in a taxi near our building. On the second day, she got into her little car and drove to a building on Rue de Longchamp, where no one of our acquaintance lived.

It was three o'clock. I waited until five. It was Cornille who came out first.

It was a situation that has given rise to much drama and, above all, to comic plays and funny cartoons in the newspapers. She emerged a quarter of an hour later.

"What an afternoon. It's getting more and more difficult to find ready money. . . ."

He never wondered why I looked at him so coldly. That evening, Anne-Marie lay down quite naturally in our bed.

"You admit," the examining magistrate insisted, "that a week elapsed between this discovery and your crime?"

I was forced to admit it, since I'd happened upon a conscientious taxi driver, who, after seeing my photograph in the papers, had rushed to a police station to make a statement.

This is very important. Well, it was important at the

163

time. My lawyer, Maître Forniol, who received me the other day as if I had the plague, gave me, when I was in Santé prison, a little lecture on the Penal Code. I still know two articles by heart:

Art. 295: Homicide committed voluntarily is termed manslaughter.

Art. 296: Manslaughter committed with premeditation or malice aforethought is termed willful murder.

"For a whole week, then, you had leisure to reflect, you gave mature consideration to your decision."

And while a prison van took me daily to the Palais de Justice, the Trade Tribunal declared the bankruptcy of La Tour Building Society and of my construction firm, thus freezing all our property.

"Why did you wait so long?"

"I don't know."

"Did the urge to kill occur to you on the first day?"

The true answer is no, and I admit it here for the first time. I lied to the judge, and then to the jury, though it did not prevent a sort of uneasiness from hanging over the whole trial.

"You are jealous by temperament?"

"Yes, Monsieur President."

"Your behavior was occasionally violent?"

"Yes."

"Toward your wife?"

"Only with her."

"Why?"

"Because I loved her."

Forniol lectured me.

"That's the crucial point. Premeditation means the death sentence. Otherwise, it's forced labor for a number of years."

I had, sometime in the past, found among my father's belongings an old repeating revolver. Anne-Marie gave evidence in the witness box without once looking at me. She was not put under oath. Nor was Monique, who glanced furtively at me, as if something was worrying her.

"On the contrary, this week of waiting, this long week of conflict and anguish seems to me to offer proof of my client's sincerity. . . . Under the shock of his discovery he remained stupefied. . . . Little by little, as hours and days elapsed, and as he watched his wife, saw how she lied while laughing and playing with the children . . ."

It was on a Friday that I made my way to Rue de Longchamp with the big revolver in my pocket. The bachelor apartment was on the ground floor and looked out on the courtyard, where a chauffeur was washing down a tenant's Rolls-Royce with a hose.

I pushed the bell, a little bone button like any other, and waited with my right hand in my pocket. I waited for some time. I could hear steps inside, the characteristic sound of bare feet.

Cornille, wearing nothing but trousers, half opened the door, and then his jaw dropped. He had time to say, in amazement:

"You!"

I pointed the gun at him, and, before I fired, he opened his mouth once more. I could read on his lips the word he was trying to call out:

"No!"

I fired three bullets, point-blank. I would have emptied the weapon if it had not jammed. I caught sight of Anne-Marie running naked through the room.

The concierge watched me go past with more curiosity

165

than alarm. She was the first person to look at me in that special way. I went to the police station on Rue de la Pompe.

"I have just killed my wife's lover."

Maître Forniol whispered to me, during the indictment:

"The president doesn't like you. . . ."

Already!

"But you'll see; the jury will react favorably. They always do, in Paris, in cases of flagrante delicto."

The jury did. They did not find malice aforethought. Recognizing, moreover, that there were extenuating circumstances, they reduced my sentence to five years.

I was almost sincere. My voice quavered when I spoke of Anne-Marie.

Today, Monday, when I went back to my job at the bookshop, and Madame Annelet looked at me with her clairvoyant's eyes, I was on the point of saying to her:

"You needn't hunt any further!"

For she is still chasing after a truth that eludes her.

"Anne-Marie had nothing to do with it. It's even possible that I never loved Anne-Marie. I believed I did. I made myself believe it. Because . . ."

My God, because, like everyone else, I needed someone, someone who belonged to me. But she did not belong to me, any more than Philippe and Nicole do. Nobody belongs to anyone else. Monique has given me further proof of that, although from her I asked nothing. Nobody has pity on anyone else, either.

In prison, one has plenty of opportunity to think. At Melun, this was particularly so in the library, where I had my own little habits, my routine, just as I have here, and where I could at last begin to take a look at myself.

I lied to all of them, not so much to avoid a severer sentence, as from fear of admitting the truth to myself. During the preliminary investigation and the trial, I had succeeded in concealing it from myself, in almost completely wiping from my memory the incident that had occurred on that Wednesday, on the Champs-Elysées.

The previous Friday, I had seen Fernand Cornille and then Anne-Marie coming out of the building on Rue de Longchamp. On Saturday evening, the four of us had gone out together. On Sunday, we went to the races. On Monday and Tuesday, I spent most of my time on the building sites.

On Wednesday afternoon, I went to the Champs-Elysées office, intending to see Mimieux; I needed money to pacify a supplier who was threatening me. I went through the reception room and the secretary's room. Mimieux's door was ajar, and just as I was about to push it open, I overheard Cornille remark:

"Allard? I'm not worrying about him. He's a weak, conceited fool; he'll go on doing whatever we decide . . ."

I retreated, on tiptoe.

"I'll come back later," I told the receptionist.

That was the heart of the matter. I understood, there, on the other side of that door, that I had just heard the truth. I had got it, as they say, right between the eyes.

Only, he had no right to say it. He had no right to rob me of my dignity, my self-esteem. Nobody has the right to do that, because without self-esteem a man ceases to be a man.

I know I behaved in the same way with Anne-Marie

in the early days, when, in my fits of jealousy, I heedlessly abused her. But she never believed me.

I believed Cornille. I knew the truth. He forced me to know it.

The rest doesn't matter. I don't care whether he waited for months or for years in a bachelor apartment on Rue de Longchamp to enjoy Anne-Marie's body.

What he stole from me was not my wife, but my self.

I will not revert to this. I will close this notebook once and for all. And I will not even kill myself. The two tubes of pills will go down the toilet.

I can't help it if people have to watch me decomposing more or less slowly, and if someday, in a hospital, I give trouble to nurses and doctors.

We are all robbers. We all steal lives, or parts of lives, to feed our own lives.

The half-empty bottle no longer tempts me.

Up you get, Bib, my boy! It's ten o'clock. I am not sleepy. We are both going out for a walk in the rain, and we'll turn right on Boulevard Beaumarchais, since we no longer are allowed to walk under certain windows.

That's all you want. You're wagging your tail already, you idiot!

News Item
Paris, January 13

Yesterday, at half past six in the evening, at the corner of Boulevard Beaumarchais and Rue du Pas-de-la-Mule, a man identified as Félix Allard, age 49, bookshop assistant, met his death in a street accident. He had been walking along the sidewalk, leading a small dog on a leash, and stepped off the curb to the street, where he was knocked over by a bus that he had his back to. His head was completely crushed. According to evidence received, Allard was subject to dizzy spells, and it is presumed that one of these attacks made him change his direction so suddenly that the driver of the bus was unable to brake in time.

The dog, which by a miracle escaped uninjured, has been taken to the pound.

Noland
September 25, 1963